Kingdom Keepers

SHELL GAME

BOOK FIVE

ALSO BY RIDLEY PEARSON

For a complete listing of Ridley's published books
visit www.ridleypearson.com

WITH DAVE BARRY

RIDLEY PEARSON

Kingdom Keepers

SHELL GAME

BOOK FIVE

DISNEP • HYPERION

Los Angeles   New York

The following are some of the trademarks, registered marks, and service marks owned by Disney Enterprises, Inc.: Adventureland® Area, Audio-Animatronics® Figure, Big Thunder Mountain® Railroad Disneyland®, Disney's Hollywood Studios, Disney's Animal Kingdom® Theme Park, Epcot®, Fantasyland® Area, FASTPASS® Service, Fort Wilderness, Frontierland® Area, Imagineering, Imagineers, "it's a small world," Magic Kingdom® Park, Main Street, U.S.A. Area, Mickey's Toontown®, monorail, New Orleans Square, Space Mountain® Attraction, Splash Mountain® Attraction, Tomorrowland® Area, Walt Disney World® Resort

Buzz Lightyear Astro Blasters © Disney Enterprises, Inc./Pixar Animation Studios

Toy Story characters © Disney Enterprises, Inc./Pixar Animation Studios

Winnie the Pooh characters based on the "Winnie the Pooh" works by A. A. Milne and E. H. Shepard

Printed in the United States of America
First Hardcover Edition, 2012
First Disney • Hyperion paperback edition, 2013
New Disney • Hyperion paperback edition, 2022
10 9 8 7 6 5 4 3 2 1
FAC-025438-22021

Library of Congress Control Number for Hardcover Edition: 2011038531
ISBN 978-1-368-04629-9

Visit ww.disneybooks.com
www.thekingdomkeepers.com
www.ridleypearson.com

SUSTAINABLE FORESTRY INITIATIVE

Certified Sourcing

www.sfiprogram.org
SFI-01054

The SFI label applies to the text stock

For my daughters, Storey and Paige,
and my wonderful readers—you make it magical.

A NOTE FROM THE AUTHOR

A great deal can change over the years, especially at Walt Disney World: new technologies, new attractions, and whole worlds. As a Keeper of the Kingdom, I felt so much has changed that it was time to update my stories to reflect those changes. Sometimes I changed only the name of an attraction or the description of a waiting line, but I often rewrote chapters or even whole sections of a book. The fun of that is, you are holding a new and updated Kingdom Keepers novel. (And the first editions remain available for those who like things just the way they were.)

So join the Keepers and me on new adventures inside Disney's new attractions, but following the same important mission: to prevent the Overtakers from stealing the magic and ruining the fun. Disney after dark has never been so unexpected. Enjoy!

—Ridley

1

FINN WHITMAN HELD UP three fingers, indicating he'd spotted the villains. One wore a full-length black robe with purple piping: Maleficent. The woman next to her wore a high, starched white collar. Her hair was perfect. She was the Evil Queen. Cruella De Vil wore the fur of ermine and stoat. Finn observed the three huddled together down an aisle of the library's stacks. Backstage, after-hours, in Disney's Hollywood Studios, the Imagineers' offices were home to a private archive. Finn and Willa had followed the three women, determined to discover what they wanted.

Finn and Willa were no ordinary teenagers. At the moment, they were holograms—three-dimensional projections of light. An invention of the Imagineers, the Disney Hosts Interactive (DHIs) served during the day as tour guides inside the four Walt Disney World parks.

By night, when the five teens who had been models for the DHIs went to sleep, it was a different story.

The Kingdom Keepers, a name the five had earned, often found themselves battling darker forces. The villains, witches, and dark fairies had plans to

1

destroy all things Disney. To take over the parks. Now called the Overtakers, a group led by Maleficent, Cruella, and the Evil Queen intended to destroy the joy and magic of Disney. The Kingdom Keepers couldn't let that happen.

Willa's dark, confident eyes sparkled as she waved Finn forward. Like Finn, she'd dressed all in black before she'd gone to bed, before she'd fallen asleep and had crossed over as a hologram. Like Finn, she'd awakened in Disney Hollywood Studios as a projection also wearing all black. She blended into the library's shadows.

The Evil Queen held a wand, the glowing tip of which was currently serving as a flashlight.

Finn moved down the aisle adjacent to the dark fairy and her two accomplices.

The Kingdom Keepers were sworn enemies of the Overtakers. The villains on the other side of the bookshelves were powerful, often terrifying. Finn and Willa had been ordered by a retired Imagineer, Wayne Kresky, to follow these three and find out what they were up to.

The Overtakers had been searching the stacks for the past forty-five minutes. They had no business being inside the private library. They obviously were looking to steal something.

But what?

The answer came only a minute later.

"Here!" Cruella said, her long fingernail pointing to the leather spine of what looked more like a journal than a book. "Is this not what we seek?"

Finn pressed his eyes close to the shelf and looked over the tops of books through to the other side.

Maleficent waited for Cruella to pass it to her. The dark fairy turned it over, studied it like a jeweler examines a diamond. She unstrapped the cover and opened it, revealing yellowed pages with fancy writing.

"Remarkable," Maleficent grumbled. "Such a small, ordinary thing. That it would possess such power. Who would think it possible?"

Finn shivered as he carefully slipped a three-ring notebook off the shelf. He indicated for Willa to do the same. He held the notebook in front of his chest as a shield. Willa did the same. Maybe they could deflect a spell, or a bolt of energy thrown at them. Willa moved down the bookshelves away from Finn.

He crept quietly to the far end of the shelving. He counted silently, giving Willa enough time to get into place.

Finn came around the end of the aisle, the binder held in front. Willa stepped into the same aisle.

Show time.

Maleficent looked over her shoulder at Finn. She glared. Finn tried hard to show no expression whatsoever.

"You can put that back," he said.

She smiled, her red lips so wet they were practically dripping with hatred.

It was always like that between her and Finn. She wanted him to mind his own business. He wanted her to play the role that had been written for her. Not the one of a revolutionary and Disney hater.

Maleficent drew back her arm like a baseball pitcher. Finn knew what was coming, but he could never match her speed. A fireball ignited on her open palm. He was her target.

A hologram couldn't be hurt by a fireball. It would simply fly through the projection. The bigger problem for Finn was that the holograms were not perfect. Fear could turn a DHI hologram more material, more solid. In this state one's hologram could be injured or hurt. Or killed.

He lifted the binder higher, prepared to deflect the fireball.

Behind Maleficent, the Evil Queen waved her wand toward Willa.

The dark fairy's fireball *whooshed* through the air. Finn blocked it. Pieces of flame exploded off the binder.

Cruella's wand threw a long two-headed snake toward Willa. The tip of her wand no longer provided light. The aisle fell into a well of darkness.

Willa, a better athlete than Finn, met the snake with her binder and bounced it off the shelves. But the snake had served its purpose. Willa was no longer fully a hologram—she was afraid of snakes. Her hologram was now vulnerable.

Willa ran toward the three villains and away from the snake. The women had not expected this. With her focus on Finn, Maleficent didn't see Willa soon enough.

The girl threw her three-ring binder at the Evil Queen, pushed Cruella aside, and grabbed the journal. She almost made it past Maleficent. But the dark fairy caught hold of Willa's vulnerable hologram. The projection stretched. Willa's arm looked six feet long. Her shoulders widened. Willa cried out and let go of the journal. It skidded across the carpet.

"Sic 'em!" Cruella called loudly.

Finn deflected another fireball. It wasn't the smoke and flames that caused his skin to prickle— a sure sign his hologram was failing due to fear. It was the sound of dogs running. Of dogs panting. He could nearly hear them drooling.

Willa was regaining her former shape and

looking beyond Finn as she grabbed his arm amid the haze of smoke.

"Run!" she cried.

Finn saw what she saw. Not dogs. Hyenas from *The Lion King*. Vicious, sickly-looking things. Heads lowered. Eyes wild. Wet tongues flapping.

Willa was a step or two ahead of him as they approached the door. As holograms, they could in theory pass through a door, wall, library shelf. Really anything. But both knew they had suffered fear. Both knew they couldn't risk smacking into the door.

Willa reached for the doorknob. A fireball exploded against the wall. The hyenas were close now. One snapped at Finn's heel. It caught and tore a piece of his pant leg.

But there was something more. Finn sensed he had been here before. In a dream? A spell?

He and Willa were running now and there was little doubt they were losing the race. Willa had the good sense to take the stairs—it took time for dogs to learn how to climb stairs. Maybe hyenas, too.

Finn continued up the stairs behind Willa. She pushed through a set of double doors. They were outside on a balcony in the cool night air. The hyenas nosed through the doors. Growled. They grouped between the two teens at the only way back inside.

Finn and Willa were trapped.

"The Return," Willa called.

Similar to a car's keyless entry remote, Finn carried a small device in his hologram's pocket. Its central button worked as a switch to cancel their DHIs.

When their hologram projection stopped, the DHIs would wake up where they'd gone to sleep. Usually, in their beds at home. It had required time for each of the Keepers to understand what was happening when they crossed over and returned. They'd become experts at it. It was second nature to go to sleep at home and wake up in a Disney park. Returning was only a matter of pushing the button on the device.

It had to be coordinated. If Finn pressed the Return without touching Willa, or at the very least being extremely close, she would remain asleep in bed, her hologram still operative. Isolated. Alone.

Jaws snapping, the hyenas charged.

Finn grabbed for Willa's hand as they ran the length of the balcony.

But she wouldn't allow him to take her hand. "Finn! Do it! Now!"

They sprinted toward a railing. They were two stories high. Finn saw only black sky and shimmering stars.

"We're going to jump the railing!" he announced.

"What? No way!"

He reached out. Took her unwilling hand. He found the Return in his pocket.

"Please . . . no!" she shouted. "Don't do this."

But the hyenas were upon them. Finn had no choice.

"We jump on three! One . . . two . . ."

They flew over the rail.

Finn pushed the button.

2

FINN SAT UPRIGHT. He had no idea where he was. Being crossed over and then returned as a DHI was often unsettling. Like traveling in a deep dream. Even when waking from such a dream it was difficult to separate fantasy from reality.

He reached for his phone to text Willa and make sure she had returned okay. The Keepers often worked in teams of two. They always looked after each other.

His phone wasn't there.

He wasn't in bed as he should have been.

Something, everything, was drastically wrong.

He had *always* returned to his bed. His room. His home. This couldn't be happening. And yet, it was.

He looked around. That was Cinderella Castle in front of him. The Partners statue behind him. Tomorrowland to his right.

He was inside the Magic Kingdom. The same dark night. The same stars in the sky.

He studied his hands. Looked down at his legs. He was still a hologram.

What?

The Return had failed to return him.

Impossible!

A rush of terror messed up his hologram. It sparked. He was losing his projection. He drew a deep breath through his nose. Slowly released it through his mouth. Repeat. Repeat again.

This kind of thing just didn't happen. *Ever!*

He stood, feeling unsteady and shaky. His hands pulsed a blue glow. He felt a warmth throughout. He was pure hologram again.

His first thought was that the Overtakers had done this. That they had gotten control of the DHI computer that controlled the projections. That they were going to kill him.

* * *

One thing all the Keepers had learned: The parks at night could be dangerous. Many Disney characters sided with the Keepers. If Finn kept his wits about him, he could find help.

He didn't love the idea of walking down Main Street, U.S.A., but it was the only way to reach the Engine Co. 71 firehouse. Wayne lived there. Wayne would help him.

"You too?" The sound of Willa's voice flooded Finn with relief. She stepped out from behind the Partners statue. "What's going on, Finn? How is this possible?"

"No idea."

"Do you still have the Return in your pocket?"

Why hadn't he checked that? He patted his pocket, then reached down into it. "Yeah!"

"Should we try again?" Willa asked. "I'd much rather be home in bed than here."

"I think we should wait," Finn said. "I don't know why, but that's what I think."

They both heard the hiss of the Walt Disney World Railroad. The cry of its engine. Willa looked confused, even scared.

"Please, Finn. Return us. Now," she said.

"The train running when the park is closed means something," Finn said.

"It means someone is in the park doing something they shouldn't be doing. Return us, please, Finn!"

"The Return didn't work, Willa. We both should be home. We aren't. Think about that."

Along with Philby, Willa got the best grades of the five Keepers. Philby was science and math. Willa won reading awards and school spelling bees.

She did think about that. "The Overtakers are controlling the server," she whispered.

"Maybe. Yes," Finn said.

"Walt Disney loved trains," she said.

"Exactly. It could be a signal *for us*."

"We have to be careful. Nothing stupid," Willa said. "If it's some kind of trap, we risk using the Return. Promise me, Finn."

"I promise. That's a good plan."

Together, they hurried toward the train's Main Street station.

As they climbed the stairs to the station platform, the train was already leaving.

"Decision time," Finn said.

"We go for it," Willa said. "But remember, you promised." Together, they jumped onto the moving train.

The train chugged away from Main Street. Finn looked around. Empty. He saw only the engineer's back, up in the locomotive. The train reached a slow but steady speed. Finn and Willa ducked as the engineer climbed out of the locomotive and headed back toward them.

"What's going on?" Willa whispered.

"No idea."

"You think he saw us?"

"Maybe."

"Get us out of here, Finn."

"Not yet."

The engineer struggled to throw a leg over the wall of the passenger car.

"He doesn't exactly look like a threat," Finn said.

"And the Overtakers have never tricked us," Willa said sarcastically.

"Wait a second," Finn said, stepping forward. "It's him!"

Wayne Kresky was old enough that he never looked older. He simply looked different wearing a train engineer's overalls and cap. His wispy white hair flew around in the breeze.

Since the first time Finn had met the man, on a bench in Town Square, Wayne had never been one for small talk. He could be difficult to understand. He could talk in circles. Without meaning to he could make Finn feel dumb or unappreciated. Most of all, Wayne was honest.

"Apologies if I've given you a shock," Wayne said; he strained to make his voice rise above the noise of the train. "I couldn't send you home just yet."

"They stole a journal," Finn said.

"Who?" Wayne asked.

Willa approached and stood alongside Finn.

Finn told the man what had happened in the library.

"Who is driving the train?" Willa asked.

"No need to worry about that, Isabella," said Wayne. "It's on tracks. It pretty much drives itself."

Willa did not look relieved to hear this.

Finn wasn't sure he'd ever heard Willa called by her given name. *Isabella*, he thought.

Wayne then described the journal in perfect detail. "Is that the one they took?"

Finn said, "So, you know what it is."

"I do."

"And it's important," Finn said.

"Every document, book, notebook, and binder in that library is important, Finn. The one you describe is an interesting choice, I must say. It's old. Very old. And while most of it is no longer relevant, there is a short section in the middle that I can assume might be of interest to the dark fairy and her kind. Yes," he said, seeming to be talking to himself. "Isn't that interesting?"

The train lurched slightly. They all reached to hold on.

"The piece you describe is an Imagineering journal from the 1940s."

Disney Imagineers—who combined skills of imagination and engineering—designed and built every attraction in every Disney park. They were dream builders.

"Why would Maleficent want it?" Finn asked.

"The journal contained some preliminary story ideas for both *Pinocchio* and *Fantasia*. You know the film *Pinocchio*. The book it is based on is a little more complicated than the film. It contains the Blue Fairy. Pinocchio's true journey is more difficult, his fate much darker than the film."

The train continued on the track, circling the Magic Kingdom. Wayne paid no attention to it.

"What about *Fantasia?*"

"As to that," Wayne said, "well, that is far more interesting to us all. You included."

Two animals leaped onto the moving train. They were nothing but blurs. Finn instinctively moved in front of Wayne to protect the man.

Willa crouched, facing the back of the train.

A fox poked its head up over a bench. The thing was so cute it was hard to take it as any kind of threat. But Finn had learned to trust nothing.

Next, a cat appeared, bounding from one seat to the next.

The fox bared its teeth and hopped up over the bench seat, now a bench closer.

The cat slinked toward Finn and Willa.

"How do you want to handle this?" Finn asked.

Wayne spoke calmly. "You're the leader."

"Not with you around I'm not," Finn said.

"Now and always," Wayne said. "We have great plans for you, Finn."

This was no time to discuss Finn's future. "Do you happen to know these two?" Finn asked.

"Not by name. But seeing as how we were discussing Pinocchio, it is a fox and a cat that led the wooden boy astray."

Finn was supposed to believe that just by talking about a story, characters within the story had come to life? He thought no sane person could possibly believe such a thing. But then who would believe a kid could go to sleep and wake up as a hologram?

"Willa, you block the cat," Finn said. "I'll take the fox."

"They are here for me," Wayne said. "I suggest you two jump and leave me to deal with them."

"Yeah?" Finn said. "Well, I'm the leader here."

The cat stretched and looked in the direction of the fox. Wayne was a good five feet from both animals.

The fox jumped at Finn. Willa moved to intercept the cat.

Finn swung hard, connected with the fox, and nearly knocked it off the train. The fox squealed.

Willa had miscalculated. The cat sprang and ricocheted off the train car's low sidewall, sidestepping her. It aimed at Wayne.

Finn stuck his leg out and tripped the cat. The fox snapped for Finn's throat, spraying drool. It meant to kill him. Another snap, too close to Finn face. Its jaws clapped as it bit through the hologram.

Wayne backed away and awkwardly climbed into the forward car.

The fox slinked toward Finn, its eyes devilish. It jumped. Finn caught the fox by the scruff of the neck. He dropped the animal over the side. It bounced, landed on its feet, and disappeared into the landscaping.

Willa cried out. "Finn! The cat!"

A shudder passed up Finn's legs. The train was speeding up. A quick look past Willa confirmed the impossible: The cat was sitting up in the locomotive. It was running the train.

The ride felt unsteady and wobbly.

"She's not built for this," Wayne called out.

On the next turn, the train's wheels lifted off the track. As it passed Space Mountain, the metal twisted and cried out. Finn passed a terrified Wayne.

"It's too fast, Finn. Too old. Too fast."

"I'm on it!"

Finn slipped between the locomotive and the car behind it. He worked the heavy iron clamp that joined the two train cars together. The train jolted. Finn lost his balance and would have fallen, but his shirt caught on something.

He looked up. Willa was bent toward him and holding his shirt.

"Thanks," he called over the roar.

Finn pulled once more. The connector released. Finn unhooked a safety chain and the cars separated.

The cat and the locomotive pulled ahead without the rest of the cars. Without Finn, Willa, and Wayne.

Once the cars came to a stop, Finn helped Wayne down. In the distance a screech of metal rang out.

"Those would be the brakes," Wayne said. "Sounds like the cat came to its senses."

"A cat," Willa said in complete disbelief.

"The power of a spell should never be under-estimated."

Wayne led them backstage near Tomorrowland.

They found some chairs and sat down.

"They were after you," Finn said.

"Apparently. Yes," Wayne replied. "The Overtakers are efficient. They will start at the top and work their way down the chain of command."

"You need to go into hiding," Willa told Wayne.

"That is an option we cannot afford right now, Isabella. There is much to accomplish."

"We're outnumbered and tired," Finn said.

"I understand that," Wayne said, "but more is being asked of you. The Overtakers work to be one step ahead. So, what's comes next for you five?"

Finn and Willa concentrated. Willa said, "The cruise. Our DHI guides are being added to the Disney Cruise Line."

"Brava," Wayne said. "Which takes us back to *Pinocchio* and *Fantasia*."

"Not sure this is the best time for a history lesson. We were just attacked by a man-eating fox and a cat that can drive a train." Finn couldn't disguise his frustration.

Wayne ignored him. Nothing new there. "*Fantasia* was the only film that Chernabog appeared in. Walt Disney referred to Chernabog as Satan himself. He's been described as part Minotaur, part Mayan bat god. He can summon fire and control ghosts and harpies. He's a creature of confusion and chaos. He is considered the most powerful villain Walt Disney ever created."

"Fascinating," Finn mumbled. He wanted sleep. He wanted to return.

"Do you know what torpor is?" Wayne asked.

"It sounds like some kind of disgusting food," Willa said.

"It is a hummingbird's resting state. Typically adopted during overnight hibernation. The Imagineers believe that Chernabog has been and is in torpor. We've expected more trouble from him than we've had. So, where's he been?"

Finn said, "You lost me."

Willa nodded. "Same."

"The journal you witnessed being stolen may contain an incantation, a conjuring. Our concern is that it may have something to with Chernabog regaining his former powers, his place as lord of the villains."

"Lord of the villains," Willa muttered. "Not loving the sound of that."

"The journal is like some kind of owner's manual?" Finn asked.

Wayne chuckled. "Could be. We won't know until you get it back."

"Excuse me?" Finn said.

"Why is it you think I interrupted your return?" Wayne said.

"To scare us?" Willa said.

"You will have a partner on the ship," Wayne said.

"Why the ship?" Finn said.

"We have observed allies of the Overtakers. These include those whom you call the Overtaker Kids. We have information that Maleficent, possibly others, is planning to stow away on the ship."

"Why would she do that? You're keeping something from us," Willa said bravely.

Wayne studied her and smiled. "You always were the smart one. Very well. What I'm going to tell you now, you never heard from me. The DHI server has been hacked, the code stolen."

"No way!" Finn said.

"We believe the villains intend to be on the cruise."

Finn couldn't breathe. He choked out. "Not possible."

"A bit of a predicament," Wayne said.

"What do we do about it?" Willa asked.

Wayne said, "You must prepare for the cruise. You must get the journal back before Maleficent uses it or whatever she has planned."

"Chernabog," Finn whispered.

"If you can't get the journal back, you must destroy it. You understand that, I'm sure."

"We understand," Willa said.

"Very well. I suggest you use the Return, Finn."

Finn felt hit in the gut. "Are you saying I could have returned us all along?"

"Yes," Wayne said, smiling. "But what would have been the fun of that?" He hesitated. "I repeat: Destroy it if you have to."

Finn grabbed hold of Willa's hand. He reached into his pocket, withdrew the Return, and pushed the button.

3

FINN OPENED HIS EYES. His bedroom was dark. It smelled like a locker room. A shape loomed alongside him. The shape was a person. The person was holding him down by the shoulders.

Finn recognized the kid pinning him as Greg Luowski. The resident bully of middle school and ninth grade, the round-faced, wet-lipped, mean-spirited boy took pleasure dishing out pain to others.

Finn saw the bedroom window was open. Luowski had snuck into Finn's bedroom.

There was someone else in the room, too. He? She? The person was holding a hose. The hose was down Finn's throat.

Finn took it all in. He'd been awake less than two seconds.

The hose connected to a funnel. A liquid, a fluid, was being poured down Finn's throat.

Finn bucked and nearly got free. A surprised Luowski climbed over him and held him down.

"Hold him still!" Luowski whispered to the other person.

Finn had never tasted booze, but he'd smelled it on his grandfather. They were pouring spirits down Finn's throat. Nasty stuff. He closed his throat and coughed. Spit the booze onto his pillow.

Luowski slapped his thick hand onto Finn's forehead and held him down.

If Finn didn't get out of this, his parents would find him drunk. They would never believe his explanation. Still held down, Finn wrapped his lips tightly around the tube. He exhaled sharply. Whatever was in the funnel sprayed into Luowski's face.

The big thug jerked back.

Finn sat up, breaking free, wondering how his parents could be sleeping through the attack.

Finn drove his heel between Luowski's legs. The boy's face brightened. His eyes bulged. Finn elbowed the guy holding the funnel.

Not a guy. It was a girl named Sally Ringwald. Both she and Luowski were known to spend time with the Overtakers. They were two of the kids the Keepers called OTKs—Overtaker Kids.

Finn came off the bed. He grabbed Sally as Luowski was about to hit him.

He hit Sally instead. She *woofed* as the air belched out of her.

Finn's mother swung open the door.

"Lawrence Finnegan Whitman!" she said, seeing him alone with a girl.

She switched on the overhead light.

Luowski took that as his cue to dive out the open window. They heard a thud. It was Luowski rolling off the roof and into bushes.

Mrs. Whitman hollered, "Is that alcohol I smell? What are the three of you up to?"

"Overtakers, Mom. OTKs. That was Luowski. You know Sally. They were trying to poison me."

"As if, Mr. Party Boy!" Sally said. The girl winced as Finn tightened his hold on her.

"Tell her," Finn said. "I was crossed over, Mom. If they'd gotten me drunk, I probably couldn't have returned. I'd be stuck in the Magic Kingdom as a hologram."

Finn and his mother often strategized together. Given that his mother had worked as a rocket scientist, he trusted her plans. She had helped Finn and the Kingdom Keepers to upset the villains' power play. She acted at times as if she hardly knew anything about the Keepers. But it was only an act.

His mother eased the door shut gently. She didn't want to wake her husband.

"Sally," Mrs. Whitman said, "should I call the police?"

"No!" Sally and Finn said in unison.

"Sally is going to cooperate," Finn said. "She's going to explain everything, aren't you, Sally?" He wrenched her arm again, enjoying it just a little too much. "Lock the door, Mom. Then lock the window. If she tries to escape, I'll tackle her."

His mother nearly objected. Instead, she did as Finn asked.

Finn released Sally. The girl sat down on the bed.

"Who sent you?" Finn asked.

Sally shook her head. Said nothing.

"My mother will call the police," Finn said.

"You wouldn't dare. That would mean the newspapers and stuff, and the Disney Hosts Interactive would be canceled." She seemed so smug.

"Bring it on," Finn said.

"Where did you get the alcohol?" Mrs. Whitman asked.

Sally turned a pasty white. "My mother and father. They keep it over the fridge."

"So, I *should* give her call," Mrs. Whitman said.

"No! Please!"

"It's late, Sally. You need to get talking."

"Luowski told me what to do. When to meet him."

"You came here knowing you were going to hurt Finn." Mrs. Whitman was about to boil over.

"No. I mean, yes. I guess."

"There are more Green Eyes than ever," Finn said. "How is that possible? We know the villains are no longer recruiting Overtaker Kids in the parks. Not at school. So how?"

"There's an online video. Greg sends out the link to all sorts of kids."

"Show me!" Finn said, pointing to his computer.

Sally hesitated.

"Now!" Finn's mother ordered.

Both Sally and Finn jumped. Sally crossed the room and used Finn's laptop to play the video.

Pictures inside the four Disney World parks played. A pair of teenage voices spoke over the images.

"Are you tired of the Disney Hosts? Had enough of all the fake smiles? It's about time the Kingdom grew up. Darkened up a bit. Became more real. More interesting. Think about it: The same people have been in charge for over fifty years. What's with that?

"Did you know that some of your favorite villains are rebelling?

"If you'd like to see things differently, you and your friends can join us. You won't be sorry. Enrollment is free and the benefits immediate. You will be trained. Assigned missions. You will be a part of the future. Click the link below to submit your application."

For a moment, Finn and his mother said nothing.

"That's lame," Finn said. "You faked that."

Mrs. Whitman leaned into Sally's face.

"Listen up, young lady. You broke into my home," she said. "You tried to poison my son. Your fingerprints are all over that stuff," she said, pointing to the funnel and tube. Sally began crying. "There's going to be alcohol in Finn's stomach. These are felonies, Sally. People go to prison for less than this."

Sobs. Sniffles. Tears.

Finn said to Sally, "The Keepers don't poison people. We don't sabotage rides or sneak into people's houses."

"We have an offer to make you," Mrs. Whitman said.

Finn wondered what she was up to.

Sally raised her head. Her tear-streaked face and grim expression told him his mother had gotten through. "Leave me alone," Sally said.

"Not a chance. I will offer this only once," his mother told Sally. "First, you're going to tell Greg Luowski that you escaped right behind him. Do you understand?"

Sally nodded.

"Second, from now on you will be spying for us," Mrs. Whitman said. "Working for us."

Us was all Finn heard. His mother was all in.

"Anything you're asked to do by Greg or others, anything you're told, you will tell Finn. Any missions. Rumors. Any anything. If I think you are lying or avoiding Finn or me, your parents will hear about it. This evidence will be brought to the police. Is that understood?"

Finn swelled with pride. *Genius!*

Sally nodded and whined. "I don't hear all that much about stuff," she choked out. "For real."

"You will now. You will make it your business to hear everything. And don't think for one minute you're the only spy working for us," Mrs. Whitman warned. Finn marveled at her ability to lie so effortlessly. He looked at his mother completely differently. He swelled with pride. "Don't think you can play with me, young lady. You'll regret that."

Sally nodded again. "I understand. I'm sorry, Mrs. Whitman." She looked up at Finn. "I'm sorry for what I . . . what we tried to do to you."

"Do what she says," Finn told her. "My mother means it."

"I get that. Yeah."

"If you betray us," Mrs. Whitman said, "you will regret it. And remember, you tell Luowski you escaped. None of this ever happened."

4

SECOND PERIOD, Willa and Finn found themselves together in History. Both wanted to discuss Finn's bedroom attack. He had texted the Keepers about it. But Mr. E. didn't appreciate "background noise."

Mr. Eisenower consistently won Edgewater High's annual "Best Teacher Award," which at least made the class tolerable. Today's class had been on the origins of mythological creatures.

Mr. E. narrated a PowerPoint slide show of all sorts of weird and twisted beasts created in mythologies in places like Indonesia, Greece, and Africa. It was one of those blocks where no one fell asleep. Nearing the end of the period, he showed a picture of Camazotz, the Mayan bat god. Both Willa and Finn gasped from opposite sides of the room.

Mr. E., who could put up with all sorts of distractions, did not appreciate being interrupted. Ever.

"Mr. Whitman? Miss Angelo? Something you'd like to share with us?"

"No, sir!" Finn answered.

"Let me have both your phones, please."

The class *oohed* and stirred. A teacher reading through one's texts promised ridicule. Social life disaster. Romantic embarrassment. Detention.

"But—"

"Now!" Mr. E. extended his hand.

"I wasn't texting *him*!" complained Willa, hoping to take the pressure off Finn. The girls in the class giggled.

"I don't want to hear it! And if I see your hand anywhere near that keypad, Mr. Whitman, it's a week of detention." Another collective gasp rose from the class.

Finn dragged himself to the front of the room. His texts had nothing to do with girlfriends, but he didn't want Mr. E. reading about Luowski and Sally Ringwald attacking him.

"I give you my word, Mr. E. I wasn't texting anyone. I was just . . . scared," he lied. "That's all. Comatose looks way creepy."

"Camazotz," Mr. E. said, correcting Finn.

The class guffawed.

"Me too," Willa said from her desk.

Mr. E. placed Finn's phone on his desk. He didn't look at it or ask for Finn's password.

Eventually the bell rang. The students left the classroom. All but Finn and Willa. Mr. E. said, "Don't you have to be somewhere?"

"Study hall," the two said, nearly in unison.

"If you're expecting your phone back, Finn, you can come by at the end of school. Same for you, Isabella."

"Actually, Mr. E., I was wondering if I could look at your PowerPoint for a minute."

"What do you mean by 'look at'?"

"I'd like to combine—"

"Two of the images," Willa said, interrupting Finn.

Mr. E. looked distrustfully between the two teens. "Be my guest," he said, motioning to the classroom computer.

Finn typed and used the trackpad.

"On the left, the Minotaur," Finn said. "On the right, Camazotz. And now—"

The images merged. Half bull, half bat.

"OMG," Willa blurted out.

"What is it?" Mr. E. said.

"Not what, but who," Finn said.

"That's Chernabog," Willa gasped.

5

MAYBECK LIVED WITH his aunt Bess above Crazy Glaze, her paint-your-own-pottery shop. The place was old and in need of repair. Coming home from school, he headed around back and bounded up the stairs. Off the kitchen was a storage room that held two small kilns and shelves of pottery. Maybeck yanked open the refrigerator and ate leftover chicken.

He and Jelly—his nickname for his aunt because she was sweet and always smelled good—worked as a team. Typically, while he struggled through homework, she watched *Jeopardy!* But on Wednesdays the store stayed open late.

Maybeck heard one of the customers asking for the bathroom.

The sound of the boy's voice triggered alarm in Maybeck. He wasn't sure why.

Yes, the small room where Maybeck stood was wall-to-wall steel shelves stacked with pottery. A large worktable occupied its center, making it tight and difficult to move. But the bathroom was *before* this workroom. Why should Maybeck feel threatened? Nonetheless, he did, and he waited to hear the bathroom door open and close.

And waited. And waited.

Greg Luowski stepped through the curtain separating the shop from the back room. The same Greg Luowski who had tried to poison Finn.

Maybeck tensed. When a second, smaller boy followed Luowski through the curtain, Maybeck spoke.

"You just passed the bathroom. Other side of the curtain."

Luowski's harsh green eyes never left Maybeck as the smaller boy turned around, allowing Luowski to reach into the boy's backpack. The smaller kid was unfamiliar to Maybeck, but that didn't matter. He was definitely an OTK. He and Luowski were there for a reason. They wanted to hurt Maybeck. To punish him for being a Keeper. Just like they had tried with Finn. Luowski removed two identical tools from the backpack. Black, with yellow plastic. He handed one of them to the guy.

"Other side of the curtain," Maybeck repeated.

"Yeah," Luowski said, "I don't think so."

Maybeck reached for a platter on the worktable. He raised it like a shield. Were those water guns Luowski and the kid were holding?

Luowski pulled the trigger and fired.

Not a water gun. Something zoomed at Maybeck. Not a bullet, but something attached to wires.

The platter shattered. Pieces rained down onto the floor. The wires connected to a piece of plastic. A stun gun, Maybeck realized. Luowski had just tried to Taser him.

"Wait!" Luowski shouted at his accomplice, who was taking aim.

At the sound of breaking pottery, Maybeck's aunt Bess pushed through the curtain.

"Terry? Everything all—? What's going on here?"

Luowski's sidekick turned toward Bess and, without thinking, pulled the trigger.

Maybeck's aunt sank to the floor. Luowski cussed. The sidekick dropped the Taser as if it was hot. Maybeck heard his aunt call his name as she fell. She hit the floor hard.

Luowski moved like a Weedwacker through tall grass. A flurry of arms and fists and kicking legs. Boys pushing other boys. Pottery fell off the shelves and exploded. Luowski found himself lying amid shards of pottery.

Maybeck slammed the other kid.

Bess mumbled Maybeck's name, calling for help.

Maybeck turned. Luowski and the kid crawled toward the back door, stood, and ran.

Customers pushed through the curtain.

"It's a heart attack!"

"She fainted!"

"I hope it's not a stroke!"

Maybeck called 911.

He waited by her side. Just before the ambulance arrived, she came awake. Bess knew a lot about her nephew's involvement with the Kingdom Keepers.

She looked up at Maybeck. "I'll tell them I fainted."

Maybeck kissed her with tears in his eyes. "I'm so, so sorry," he said. "This will never happen again."

Deep within Maybeck a storm was brewing. Luowski and the Overtakers had brought the fight into his home.

You have crossed a line, he thought.

6

JESS AND AMANDA lived with their foster mother, Mrs. Nash, along with a handful of other girls. Considered runaways, the two friends were, in fact, escapees. Two years earlier they had fled a government institution that called itself a boarding school. Set on an unused army base near Baltimore, the Barracks tested and experimented on children with unusual abilities.

Jess rolled over in the lower bunk and reached for her sketch pad. It served as her dream journal. She drew a dark room with fabric walls and a floor painted black. There was a large wooden crate in the room, men in overalls, and a friend of hers. Charlene, one of the Kingdom Keepers.

Amanda's face appeared upside down from the overhead bunk. "Another one?"

Jess spoke softly. "This one was vivid. I was right there. It was Charlene. There was a box. A crate. A big crate."

Jess went quiet. It wasn't like her. Amanda slipped off the bunk and sat alongside Jess, facing her. She stroked Jess's hair. It was coarse. Jess dyed it a dark brown, almost black. Without the coloring her hair was nearly pure white—the result of being held captive by Maleficent for nearly a year. Jess had never fully recovered from that year of horror.

"It's all right," Amanda said. "Maybe don't think about it."

"I have to tell them," Jess said. "The Keepers. I have to tell them."

"About the box?"

"Not the box." Jess fought back tears. "It wasn't the box that scared Charlene. It was what was in it."

7

THE CODE CAME THROUGH the Cast Member's Wave Phone. She had not been expecting it, but she'd been prepared. Trained. Made ready. She read it twice to make sure. There was no question about it. She was being put into service. She stepped outside onto the ship's deck. Waves crashed against the hull some forty feet below. The horizon was strong, the sky clear. Tears of joy filled her eyes. If anyone came along, she would say it was the wind in her eyes.

She replied with the proper code of acknowledgment. She accepted the assignment. Within hours, a day at the most, she would be sent a highly secure email with the rest of the details.

It was most likely a VIP coming on board the ship. She would take care of this person. It might even be a Disney executive, in which case the meeting could be even more exciting. Several possibilities filled her imagination. The best job ever would be to spy on a guest or another Cast Member. Learning those skills had been the most fun during training. Only two of the Cast

Members accepted for the program had been quali-
fied for surveillance. She was proud to be one of them.
She told herself it didn't matter what assignment was
offered. She'd been activated.

Something new and different was coming her way.

8

THE LIVING ROOM CURTAINS rustled as an evening breeze created a gentle flapping sound, like a dog scratching at the door. There was no other sound in the room except for Finn's breathing. He awaited his mother's decision. He had offered a proposal, one that had bothered her. If she wouldn't help him, then he'd have to lie to her. He'd never done that. When his mother was upset, her face became pinched and puckered. She looked like a bird.

"If you're going to ask this of me," she whispered harshly, "couldn't you at least make the request reasonable?"

"You want me to tell Wayne I won't do it? He'll just ask Philby or Willa or someone else, and how is that fair to them?"

"You're playing with me," she said. "Watch it."

Busted, he thought. Not much got past his mother.

She raised her voice. "I helped you in Hollywood Studios, let's not forget. I thought that would be the end of it."

"Everything all right in there?" Finn's father called

from the television room. Finn's little sister moved about like a ghost. She was probably in her room. Half the time he forgot she lived there.

"We're fine!" his mother called out. She spoke to her son. "We'll have to think up an excuse," she whispered. "He's not stupid, you know."

"What about something to do with SuperBuy?" Finn's father was consumed with the SuperBuy website. He was buying stuff he had no use for simply because it was 70 percent off.

"You really did inherit my brains," his mother said. "I'll tell him there's a sale on kids' clothing at Downtown Disney. That'll do it."

His mother leaned her head into the television room. "There's a later-night pop-up sale in Downtown Disney. Finn and I will be back in an hour or so. Make sure the little one gets to bed on time."

His father grumbled.

A few minutes later Finn and his mother were in the car. Finn told his mother to shut her eyes so he could change into his bathing suit.

"I can't shut my eyes! I'm driving."

He climbed into the back and changed, then returned to the front passenger seat.

"I don't want you going in the water," his mother said.

"Typhoon Lagoon is a water park, Mom."

"Don't get smart with me."

"I'm just saying I want to be ready."

"But you'll be careful."

"I'm always careful," Finn said.

His mother barked out a laugh.

9

FINN HAD NEVER BEEN to Typhoon Lagoon at night. The palm trees formed a dark throat that swallowed the car. The attraction lit the night sky. It looked as if a UFO was hovering over the jungle.

"You're sure he said ten o'clock?" his mother asked from behind the wheel.

"Positive."

"It's empty?"

"It's Wayne, Mom. He does things his way." The huge parking lot held only a few cars.

"Wouldn't you be safer crossed over? As your DHI?"

His mom understood the safety advantages of the DHI hologram technology. This, even though she didn't approve of her own child using it.

"Our DHIs aren't projected here yet. Only in the parks. And then on the ships, once you and I do this cruise thing."

"Keep your phone on," she said. "I'll call you if I see anything."

"Keep the doors locked," Finn said.

"What's that supposed to mean?" she said nervously.

"These people—well, they aren't exactly people," he said. "The OTs don't play fair."

"If you're trying to scare me, it's working," she said.

"I'm trying to be smart," he said, quoting her.

"How can you get in, if it's closed?"

"There's a private party. I'm on the guest list. Wayne thinks of everything. You don't need to worry." He said good-bye and headed for the entrance.

"Aren't you—?" the Cast Member asked.

"Finn Whitman."

"One of the guides," she said a little breathlessly. He got this a lot. The DHIs—the Kingdom Keepers—had gained notoriety within the parks.

"A Disney host. Yes," he said.

"Nice to meet you." She leaned in toward him and whispered. "Listen . . . is there any truth to the—"

"Rumors, that's all," he said, cutting her off. People were always asking whether the stories about the Kingdom Keepers were true. The contract Finn and the others had signed prevented him from saying anything.

"You're welcome anytime I'm at the front," the woman said. She motioned him through the entrance.

Finn heard the party going on over at Crush 'n' Gusher. Once across the bridge over Castaway Creek, he turned left as Wayne had instructed. He continued around toward Keelhaul and Mayday Falls. As a Keeper, Finn was used to empty Disney parks. But Typhoon Lagoon was a new one for him. He walked around the surf pool. Its water was as flat and shiny as an ice skating rink.

He walked the long way around to the Typhoon Boatworks.

He took the tunnel that led to Mountain Trail and continued toward Humunga Kowabunga, his second-favorite spot in the park after StormSlides.

When he heard something, someone, behind him, he ducked into the foliage. He waited, hoping to spot the person following him. *Nothing.*

Back on the path again, he heard the same sound. Again, he hid.

The sounds grew closer. Finn tensed. There was something wrong with the way they walked, the way they sounded.

Then he spotted them. He felt a shiver. He was deathly cold.

Six rescue dummies walked past. They were for lifesaving drills, and their limbs were all messed up. Their feet pointed backward. Their arms were twisted inhumanly. They stumbled along like zombies. Four were adult size. Two children.

This was worse than *Small World.*

They were are all boys with bare plastic chests. Their "faces" were plastic heads with blank stares. Finn held his breath as they passed. After a moment he slipped quietly back out onto the path. To avoid the dummies, he climbed over some rocks and lowered himself to a stairway. He was at the entrance to Humunga. Heading toward Boatworks, he encountered a child rescue dummy coming the other way. The mutant child slapped the side of its upper leg. It rang as loud as a drum. Dummies couldn't talk, but they could send drum signals.

Finn turned and ran. He would be faster than the dummies with their crooked feet and awkward motion.

He reached the top—practically to *Miss Tilly*, the wrecked boat at the very top of the park. He faced the dark, open holes of three water tubes. He launched himself feetfirst down the middle tube. It felt more like he'd jumped out of a window. He fought to keep from shouting. Finally, the water slowed as the tube leveled.

Finn pulled himself out of the slide as two adult dummies hurried toward him.

He knew not to lead them to his meetup at the Boatworks. He lay flat on the ground. Two dummies limped past.

He tried to collect himself, to settle down. Were the dummies after him or just on patrol?

A teenage dummy arrived via a waterslide. It

spotted Finn and raised its fists. A plastic dummy couldn't be hurt. At best, Finn could knock the thing over and run. Two more dummies splashed into the slide's landing pool. It was three against one.

Just then, Finn saw a flash of blue to his right.

Stitch.

This was no costume. The character's mouth and eyes moved. His facial skin looked oily in the dim light. Stitch was not happy. His ire was aimed at the three dummies. He flashed his rows of sharp teeth.

Finn felt a chill as Stitch growled and stepped toward the dummies. They retreated. Stitch put himself between Finn and the dummies. Stitch gestured for Finn to get moving and Finn did just that. Behind him, he heard a shriek, frantic drumming, growling, and something that sounded like pain. An object flew through the air. It landed on the path in front of Finn. It was part of an arm—a torn dummy arm with a large bite mark on it.

Finn ran hard and fast, reaching the Boatworks cabin. He bent over and grabbed his knees to catch his breath.

When he looked up, he was facing a girl wearing Typhoon Lagoon Cast Member shorts and shirt. She wore her dark hair in a braid.

"I'm Melanie." She looked like she was in high

school or college. She had dark brown eyes and a wide face.

"Finn."

"Yes. I, we, so appreciate what you and your friends are doing."

"Th . . . thanks," he stuttered.

"We'll do anything to help you. Anything in our power. Seriously. The last thing we want is Maleficent as our boss."

"Overtakers," Finn said. "We call them Overtakers."

"Lilo asked me to give you this," she said, indicating a surfboard leaning against the shack. "All you will have to do is paddle. But you'll need a rash jacket, and I have a full wet suit for you if you'd rather."

"I'm going surfing?" Finn asked.

She glanced toward the Surf Pool and then at Finn. "That's what I was told. Yes. I'm supposed to get you outfitted and then clear out. Crush 'n' Gusher is shutting down for the night."

"No problem," he said.

Finn undressed down to his swim trunks. Melanie helped him into the vest. "You'll lie flat on the board with your feet hanging off the back so you can kick while you paddle. You're supposed to paddle into the middle of the tank. Face the wall and wait. If a wave comes, you'll bob up over it."

Finn thanked her again and carried the board down the stairs. He threw it in the water and jumped in after it. Across the park he saw a Cast Member leading partying kids to the exit. Party over.

Finn looked back up the steps. He was all alone.

10

THE FIRST SIGN that something was wrong was a series of pops and clunks. They came from the wall that Finn faced while floating in the Surf Pool. Those strange sounds were followed by a whoosh of water. Lots of water. He'd seen the Surf Pool in action before. First the wall made a belching sound. Next, out came waves. Big waves, eight feet high.

He spotted someone standing by the shack. He didn't like the idea of someone watching him. It creeped him out.

The wall coughed and gushed water. The huge wave was peaked in the middle, divided into two waves, each running toward the opposing side walls. The waves rose fifteen feet, bigger than anything Finn had ever seen. Sitting on his surfboard, he rose with the swell. The water smashed off the walls. It formed a white-capped boil. It came directly at Finn.

The front of his board jerked straight up. He clung to the board as it slid down the wave. The rush of water hit his face and pried his mouth open. Finn gagged and heaved. He fought to hold on. The surfboard's leash remained tight around his right ankle. The wave, pushing from behind, slipped beneath him. It crashed to shore. Slowly the water's surface calmed. Finn calmed.

But the gurgling began again. Finn paddled. Melanie had told him to face the wall. He heard a second ferocious belch. The next wave was going to be even higher than the first. It released.

Not possible, Finn thought, watching it grow.

It wasn't a wave. More like a wall of water as high as a house. It was going to own him. It was going to lift him, carry him, and crush him.

The water turned into a surging foam. Huge clumps of seaweed that did not belong in the pool rose to the surface.

Finn panicked and back-paddled. It was of no use. He was going to be swallowed whole.

Not seaweed, he realized. It was . . . hair. Massive tangles covered what looked like a stone statue. But then it wasn't stone. It was flesh. Gray flesh. An old man's eyes, nose, and beard. The water poured off the man as he seemed to rise from the water. His shoulders were revealed. A cape was tied around a strong chest and bulging, bare arms. The bearded man held a staff in one hand, a golden pitchfork in the other. *No*, Finn thought, *not a pitchfork.* It was a trident.

King Triton's trident.

A terrified Finn paddled hard to get out of the pool.

"Name yourself!" The man's voice ruffled the water, shook the pool.

There was no escaping. Finn turned the board around. He faced Triton.

"Finn," he muttered so softly he couldn't hear it himself.

"Louder! Your full name!"

"Lawrence. Finnegan. Whitman."

"State your purpose."

"Ah . . . a friend sent me." Finn was wondering why Wayne had done that.

"Indeed. A friend to us all." King Triton knew Wayne? "Our friend is the keeper of the magic," he said.

The wave smashed into the pool furniture on the beach. It crashed out to the parking lot. Triton waited before speaking.

"Our friend seeks protection for you, Lawrence Finnegan Whitman," said Triton.

"Ah . . ." Finn wasn't sure what to say. "Right!"

"For your voyage in my kingdom."

What voyage? Triton ruled the sea. Finn couldn't think clearly. A voyage.

"The cruise!" Finn shouted. "Yes, sir. Please, sir. Your majesty. Your kingship."

"My realm is vast. Unchangeable, horizon to horizon. There is much to protect. Your people poison mine. They hunt with invisible line and nets that stretch for miles. With harpoons. Oil rigs. They make war above and below."

"Yes, your majesty!" Finn said.

"I am king. And I am old. My wants are few. You, on the other hand, Lawrence Finnegan Whitman, your needs and wants are many. My agents will never be far from you and your friends. This, I promise as a favor to our mutual friend."

"Thank you, King Triton."

"The porpoises and frigate birds will observe you. When the flying fish are near, I am not far away. The spoken code is simple: 'Starfish wise, starfish cries.'"

"The code?" Finn said.

"To summon my agents. Starfish are never far away."

"Seriously?" It just slipped out. Finn hadn't meant to say it aloud.

"You will summon my help only if your situation is dire. You understand? You must speak within the water. A summons spoken in air is of no use to you."

"Water. Got it. What did you say about the frigate birds?" Finn couldn't remember things clearly. He was too much in awe of King Triton.

"You dare question my instructions? The insolence!"

The king waved his trident. A wide circle of water rose around Finn and closed at the top like the peak of a teepee, trapping Finn inside.

"I'm sorry! I'm sorry!" Finn cried out.

"Speak into the water!" the king hollered. As he lowered the trident, the peak of water, which was about to drown Finn, lowered as well.

Finn slipped his head off the board and bubbled water as he said, "Sorry! *Sorry!*"

The water funnel collapsed, smashing into Finn and knocking him off the board. He struggled back atop and held on for dear life.

"You don't apologize, Lawrence Finnegan Whiteman. You speak the code: 'Starfish wise, starfish cries,'" the king roared. "We will do everything in our power to assist or rescue you and your friends if summoned."

"Okay. I get it!" Finn said. He could hardly think, he was so scared.

"Our powers are considerable."

"And what do I do in return?" Finn asked.

Triton blinked. It sprayed Finn.

"If you're offering to protect us, is there something you want in return? Like Ursula's necklace or something."

"Do not mention her!" Triton's anger was palpable.

Finn had made a mistake. A big mistake.

The water boiled. It formed into waves with white ridges. The surfboard spun clockwise. Finn was caught in the swirl. The spiny back of a sea serpent rose from the pool. A hole opened in the water beneath him. A whirlpool started.

King Triton lifted the trident and shook the hair from his neck.

"Away from this place!" the king shouted.

Finn thought he was talking to him. But in the middle of being sucked down the whirlpool, he wasn't so certain.

"Help!" Finn gurgled.

The surfboard spun faster. Finn held on tightly.

An ugly, purple-skinned, thick-lipped woman rose out of the pool. She faced Triton. She looked part octopus, part cow. Her skin was disgusting. A spiderweb of veins pumped rust-colored blood. The skin of her face sagged.

"Who called my name?" the big blob said.

This was Ursula.

"Your presence is unwanted," Triton said.

"I didn't bring you any presents," Ursula said, twisting his words. She chuckled at her own joke, throwing three-foot waves off her belly.

Finn was now nearly to the bottom of the whirlpool. He spun on the surfboard like it was a propeller.

Through the silver walls of water, he saw squidlike creatures, manatees, and puckered fish with bulging eyes. The fish circled the whirlpool. One poked its gills through the wall of water and snapped at Finn. It bit a chunk out of the surfboard.

The sides of the whirlpool collapsed. The walls of water folded in on themselves with Finn at the bottom.

He needed a way out. Now!

He stood and pointed the nose of the surfboard into the spinning water. He rose like a screw, lifting higher.

"Leave or be removed!" Triton bellowed at Ursula.

"What'sa matter? Can't a girl have some fun? Someone invited me, don't forget. He spoke my name!"

"The summons was unintentional. You are not needed."

"Be that way," she said.

"Be gone or I will be rid of you."

"Oh, I'm quaking all over!" With that, she threw her hips around, disturbing the pool.

Finn saw more of the strange squid creatures. Ursula sank slowly in front of him. For a moment she looked directly at Finn. The entire pool began to quake. Ursula disappeared.

Triton towered above Finn. The wave wall gurgled louder than ever.

"*Go!*" Triton shouted. "I will do what I can!" He held the trident out before him as the wave wall began to break up.

Triton's effort was formidable. He held the staff before him. A hole formed in the water around him. Triton held his ground. A wave several stories high rose above the wall.

Finn reached the shallows. He climbed off the board and ran.

Behind him, the wave formed majestically, beautifully. It suddenly looked like a mouth opening. Finn continued to run in the knee-deep water. He was slow. Ursula's wave peaked. Triton was swallowed up.

The wave curled, rose, and . . . stopped. Its waters churned, but the wave did not collapse. It was suspended in place.

Finn spun around.

Amanda stood in the water. She wore a hoodie over pajamas. She was *pushing* an unseen force against the wave. Holding it from crushing down onto Finn. She had used this ability to help the Keepers many times.

"Hurry!" she said. "Grab hold of my waist!"

Finn understood the power she contained in her arms. He grabbed hold her around her waist and held tightly.

Amanda kept her arms extended. The wave grew to thirty feet. Forty. The water jumped the walls of the Surf Pool.

"Don't let go," she shouted. "Guide me toward the gate. I can't hold it."

Holding her, Finn walked her backward while Amanda remained facing the towering wave, her elbows locked.

"I'm losing it," she said.

The wave moved forward as they moved back. It matched Finn step for step.

"I can't hold it," she said. In fact, her arms were trembling, her strength waning. The wave had changed positions, now leaning like a shelf directly overhead. If it collapsed they would be drowned.

"I shall hold it!" came Triton's thundering voice. His face appeared within the towering wave. "Go! Both of you! Quickly!"

Finn kicked aside some of the tangled pool furniture, making a path.

He nudged a clear rafting tube aside.

"I've got an idea," he said.

Amanda turned as Triton held back the wall of water.

Finn tugged Amanda by the arm as he dove for a

double tube floating nearby. He pulled her into the tube with him.

The wave collapsed. It wasn't just a wave, but a flood.

The tube lifted. Finn and Amanda held the handles tightly. They lifted into the curl.

The nose of the tube broke free and fell down the steep incline of water like a sled on ice.

Down, down they raced.

They broke out into the parking lot. The water spread quickly, lowering as it did.

Knee-deep. Ankle-deep.

Finn's mom waved from inside her car.

She looked scared to death.

11

FINN WALKED AMANDA to the side of Mrs. Nash's house while his mother waited in the running car. Amanda was going to sneak back in before anyone woke up.

"How did you know to show up at Typhoon?" he asked.

"It wasn't me. It was Jess. Another one of her dreams. One of her drawings tonight had today's date on a sign."

"Out front of Typhoon Lagoon. The party." Finn had seen it, had walked past it.

"That's the one. She saw the damage from the wave." Amanda hesitated, not wanting to say what came next. "You, Finn. She saw you. I ran to a bus." Even in the dark Finn could see her beet-red face.

Finn leaned in to kiss her on the cheek as he thanked her. Amanda turned away and it ended up a kiss on the ear. "You probably saved my life," he said.

"No. I don't think so."

"You held that wave while I got out of there."

"Right place at the right time," she said.

"Did you see Triton?" he asked. Partly he wanted to

know if she had been in awe the way he had. But he also wanted to make sure he hadn't imagined what he'd seen. What had happened.

"I heard two voices. A man and a woman. Big voices. Huge voices."

"Yeah," Finn said. He wasn't going to go into details. He would sound like a maniac. *No one loves a maniac.*

"You're leaving on the cruise," she said.

"Yes. Soon."

"How would you feel if Jess and I came along?"

"I don't have that kind of pull," he said. "We all have to go with our parents. Maybeck with Bess, but same thing."

Unspoken between them was that Jess's and Amanda's parents had allowed their daughters to be put into the Baltimore boarding school. The Barracks turned out to be a place where kids with strange powers were taken. Jess and Amanda had escaped the Barracks. They couldn't call their parents to come on a cruise.

"Right," she said. But something lingered on the tip of her tongue. Something unexplained and mysterious. "I'd better get inside," she said.

Finn gave her a leg up. Amanda climbed a trellis, taking care not to squash the flowers and vines. When she reached her window, she looked down at Finn, who was looking up. There were no words spoken, but a lot was said.

"He kissed me. On the ear," Amanda told Jess as she changed into fresh pajamas.

"The better to hear you with. I have Q-tips if you need them."

"Ha, ha. Very funny." Amanda tossed her wet clothes onto the floor of the small closet. "Your dream, the sketch, was spot-on. I got there right when I had to."

"Lucky."

"It's a gift, Jess. A real gift."

"It's not like I can move a desk across the room by *pushing*," Jess said.

"To each their own."

The girls laughed.

When the lights were out and they were in the bunks, the girls couldn't stay quiet.

"I asked him about the cruise," Amanda said.

"What did he say?"

"He didn't get it. He thought I was asking him to get us invited."

"So, it'll be a surprise."

"I suppose. Yeah," Amanda said.

"What's bugging you?"

"Everything," Amanda answered. "He could have been killed tonight. First, they tried to poison him in his own bed. Then they attacked Bess and Maybeck. Now Wayne sends Finn to Typhoon Lagoon and he's nearly drowned. Again."

"Hmm," Jess said. "Do you think Wayne will pull this off?"

"Well, if he does, it's going to be a surprise. You're right about that."

"A shocker," Jess said.

The girls giggled. They said good night.

Amanda had the last word. "No more dreams tonight. Okay?"

12

THE KEY TO NOT LOOKING suspicious was posture. The girl with the black hair dyed red at the tips walked with intention, with purpose. She left the ship's elevator carrying a cardboard box that hung from a black plastic handle. About the size of a briefcase, it was heavy, and she had to pretend otherwise. As long as she kept her back straight and her head high, she looked as if she belonged here. She did not. The Radio Studio on the *Disney Dream*'s Deck 11 was intended for people with press passes or radio credentials. Only a few Cast Members, all technicians like Tim Walters and Rich Fleming, had reason to enter the studio.

She swiped her Cast Member ID and the door unlocked. She suspected that she had an Imagineer to thank for that. The new card had been slipped under the door to her ship's quarters. Her roommate had put the envelope on her pillow. To her great surprise the new card opened every door of the ship where she tried it. Now she had a card as powerful as the captain or the chief executive officer. Magic really did happen on the Disney Cruise Line.

She switched on the Radio Studio's lights and went to work. The studio's glass door and walls meant others could see in. She kept that in mind as she went about her business, despite the fact no one—absolutely no one but the press—ever had reason to be on this part of Deck 11. The press only came onto the ship for big occasions. The upcoming cruise was just such an occasion, but it didn't start until tomorrow.

On this night, the ship felt nearly empty. Only the crew and Cast Members were sleeping aboard—about fourteen hundred of the fifty-four hundred people the ship could hold.

The box pulling at her elbow contained a computer slave. It connected to the studio's existing computer system, which in turn connected to speakers and projectors all over the ship. The girl tucked it under and behind one of the large, multiperson desks used for broadcasts and recordings. She plugged in a thin cable marked FIBER to the other computer, and then the electricity to the wall. It turned on automatically, blinking red and blue for several minutes before the colorful lights stayed solid. She banged her head as she climbed out from under the desk.

She didn't know exactly what she'd just done. She wasn't sure she wanted to know. She was doing the job she'd been trained for. No questions asked. No curiosity allowed to interfere with her actions.

13

In THE GLOW of warm sunshine, a magnificent cruise ship rose fifteen stories from the water's blue surface. It towered over the four-acre cruise terminal where excited passengers awaited boarding.

Reporters with film crews crowded the VIP waiting lounge beneath a sign welcoming all to the *Disney Dream*'s Panama Canal Passage.

"Please, tell us what it's like," a Spanish-speaking reporter asked a young couple who appeared surprised by the television camera shoved in their faces.

"Incredible!" the man answered.

"What makes this trip so special when compared with other Disney cruises?" the reporter asked.

The woman answered. "We will be the first Disney ship to transit the new Panama Canal. We are living history."

"And those guides," the man said. "The Disney guides from the parks. First time they'll be on any ship."

"The Disney Hosts Interactive," the woman said. "The hologram guides. We are both big fans."

"Aren't we all?" said the reporter. "Have you been guided by the holograms in the parks before?"

"Five times!" the man answered, cutting off his girlfriend. "The absolute greatest experience ever. You can walk right through them if you like. And if you ask them a question—"

"They know all the history, all the answers," the woman said.

The reporter thanked them, waited for her cameraman to collect their gear, and moved down the waiting line, microphone at the ready.

Not far away, also in the VIP lounge, Finn, Maybeck, Philby, Charlene, and Willa waved to their fans and smiled for the cameras. Each had at least one parent along as a guardian. Maybeck had Bess. Thankfully, the parents kept their distance.

The five tour guides entered the ship's atrium. They were asked for their names so they could be announced over the loudspeaker. Their Disney publicist, Jen Levine, intercepted the announcement.

"VIPs," she told the Cast Member holding the microphone. Jen whisked away the Keepers and their parents. She bypassed the midship elevators already crowded with passengers. Herded down a long corridor and past some shops, the group reached the forward elevators. "You'll be on the Concierge level. You're going to love the rooms! There's also a private lounge just for Concierge. It's up to you how much you mingle with passengers in your downtime. Just beware, you and the DHIs are a big part of this cruise, so you may encounter more fan attention than you're used to."

"Stalkers," Maybeck said.

"I wouldn't go that far," Jen said. "Enthusiastic fans, let's call them."

"Stalkers," Maybeck repeated. Everyone laughed.

The staterooms were beyond anything that the kids or their parents had experienced. Each suite had a living room, a private verandah with balcony, two TVs, and a refrigerator. Finn's mother got the bedroom. His bed folded down from the living room wall.

"They're keeping you and the others busy," his mother called, unpacking. Finn used the hallway closet to store his suitcase. "I have a copy of your schedule."

"There's one here, too." Finn called back. He hoped she wasn't going to bug him for the whole cruise. So annoying! "And they put it on our Wave Phones, too."

"What's a Wave Phone?"

"Yours is probably by your bed. They got us a cell phone package, but the Wave Phone is a Disney thing. Each of ours has our schedule, speed dials, that stuff."

"You'll have to show me," she called. She was just being nice. Finn's mother was more of a techie than Philby.

"No problem," he said. He didn't want to lie to her. He tried to think how he could say what he had to say. "I've got to pick up some costuming from the Cast Member laundry. I'll be back in a minute."

"No problem," his mother said.

Finn hoped she was right.

14

"THAT AIN'T RIGHT," said the ship painter's helper. He was a small man with thick hands and a dark tan. "Since when do characters board the ship wearing them costumes?"

"Don't get your BVDs in a twist," the painter said from his boatswain's chair. The fabric chair hung from a pair of ropes slung through pullies overhead on the ship. He was touching up the fresh paint on the *Dream's* hull. Tall, and unremarkable looking given his narrow eyes, he spoke in a deep voice.

"I don't wear no BVDs," his helper said.

"TMI!" said the painter in the boatswain's chair. "I seen what you seen, okay? So what? Our job is to paint. Period. Leave them characters for others."

"It bothers me. Ain't seen nothing like it before."

"You can be a real knucklehead, you know that?" the painter said.

"Better than a fake knucklehead," said the helper.

The painter laughed. "Whatever that means!"

"Least I don't wear one of them Jafar costumes!"

"Yeah, seen that myself," the painter said, still laughing. "Must get hot in them costumes."

"It ain't me, that's for sure."

"You? What, as Maleficent? More like Goofy."

"Shut it."

"You shut it."

It continued like this for several more minutes. The last swipe of black paint was applied. The men began to pack up. They talked about getting to see the Panama Canal for the first time. They talked about the pretty girls on the beaches of Aruba. There was no more mention of costumes, though neither man could forget what he'd just witnessed.

15

WAYNE HAD SUPPLIED the Keepers with alias Cast Member ID cards. The *Dream*'s electronic entry system was used throughout the ship. Each unlocking of a crew door or stateroom was captured on computer. The same was true for leaving or reboarding the ship. A history, called a "manifest," was constantly maintained for every crew member, Cast Member, passenger, and ship executive.

If the Kingdom Keepers were detected unlocking secure doors, there would be trouble.

Cast Members didn't dress like the crew or the passengers. They wore a variety of outfits, usually white or khaki shorts, a dark or powder-blue polo, and white deck shoes. If they were to act as Cast Members, they had to look like Cast Members.

Cast Member laundry was exchanged within the administration area. Each piece of laundry had a tiny electronic tag sewn into it that could be scanned for checking in and checking out. Like library books.

Maybeck and Charlene might pass for eighteen,

but the other Keepers would not. Even with the alias cards, Finn, Philby, and Willa would need to be careful moving around the ship. For this reason, Maybeck and Willa were to pair up. Charlene and Philby. Finn would join either of the trios as often as possible. Maybeck and Willa were first to arrive to the laundry.

The Cast Member behind the counter wore a head scarf. Her fingernails were natural. Her only jewelry was a thin silver bracelet.

"Sarah Sandler," Willa said, passing the girl her alias card.

The girl typed. She headed back into some shelving and returned with a bundle of folded laundry wrapped in stretch wrap. No problems. Willa thanked her.

Maybeck—alias Randy Coleman—collected his own bundled clothing, also wrapped in plastic. His was white, a baker's outfit. They both returned to their staterooms and changed into the new clothes. Maybeck left first, using crew companionways and stairs to avoid the three thousand passengers who were in the process of boarding. Willa left her stateroom ten minutes later.

Maybeck followed the memorized route to the food stores on Deck 1. The area was less like a ship and more like a warehouse, though sparkling clean. He passed crates of juices, drinks, cereals, flour, oats, rice, pasta—all clear-wrapped and stacked on wood pallets. The pallets were strapped to the deck. To his right stood a long row of walk-in refrigerators and freezers. Most had their doors open, since the ship was still in the loading process. He saw fruits, vegetables, meats, a thousand fresh eggs, and cheese wheels the size of truck tires.

The mission: find and retrieve the stolen journal.

Maleficent favored cold environments. Even the slightest warmth slowed her down. She preferred night over day, Disney World over Disneyland. The coolest places for her to hide on the ship would be the food service refrigerators. It wouldn't be easy to disguise her green skin or her horns. She would likely lie low in one of the food coolers by day and come out only at night. Maybeck and Willa would have to surprise her to be successful. Maleficent would not surrender the journal without a fight.

Willa arrived wearing a paper hat to keep her hair up and a white apron over her kitchen staff costume. She and Maybeck nearly collided as he left the third walk-in refrigerator he had searched.

"Nothing," he said.

"It's too busy," Willa whispered. "She might hide around here at some point. I'll give you that. But not in this chaos."

"Or maybe one of the galleys after dinner," Maybeck said.

"That's Finn's assignment," she said.

"Yeah."

"It's still worth looking around," Willa said. "You never know."

"Not with her you don't," Maybeck said. They each took a side and continued searching.

"Don't just stand around," a balding man shouted at Maybeck. "You're baking, right? So, there's a couple hundred pounds of flour out on the dock that needs loading. Get to it!"

"Yes, sir," Maybeck said. Moving fifty-pound sacks of flour was not going to help him find Maleficent. But the supervisor was watching him now. He had no choice. He grabbed a hand truck and headed for blinding sunlight at the end of a long warehouse space.

He caught a glimpse of Willa across the way. The ship was wide enough that he'd have trouble throwing a football across it. Willa offered him a small shake of the head. *Nothing*, it told him.

Distracted by her, Maybeck's hip caught, turned him, and he dropped the hand truck. It banged loudly on deck. The supervisor hurled some unpleasant words in Maybeck's direction. Reaching for the hand truck, Maybeck saw the metal staple that had snagged him. It was bent and twisted, with a few white fibers from his costume's pants dangling. It was partially stuck into a wood pallet that had been placed awkwardly atop boxes and boxes of potato chips.

There was another piece of fabric caught on the crooked staple. It fluttered in a breeze pouring into the hold from outside. It danced like a ribbon around a pigtail.

"What the devil is taking you so long?" The supervisor marched angrily toward Maybeck.

Maybeck pinched the torn piece of fabric and wrestled it off the bent staple. He slipped it into his pocket as he stood holding the hand truck. "There's a nail or something caught me," he said.

"Oh!" The supervisor wouldn't want Maybeck filing an injury report. Not given the overly large sign that read: 235 consecutive days with NO ACCIDENTS! "You okay?"

"Fine," Maybeck said. "It only nicked me. Nothing major."

"Why don't you take five and get that cleaned up?" the man offered.

"Yes, sir. Thank you, sir." Maybeck tried to signal Willa, but her head was inside a plastic crate at that moment.

He headed toward the toilets.

He reached in and touched the piece of torn fabric just to make sure it was still there.

He'd gotten a good look at it when he was pulling it off the staple.

It was shiny black, with purple piping. That combination of colors told him it was from a woman's cape. A villain he knew only too well.

16

"IT'S STARTING," said one of the other girls, a tall, trim, sharp-nosed girl with a dancer's long legs. Charlene followed her out of the elevator and down a hall to a meeting room. A dozen Cast Members were dressed as she was dressed, in white shorts and the blue polo.

"Okay, so listen up, everyone!" The team leader was probably in the college program. "This Sail-Away is different today." Dark hair. Dark eyes. She looked and acted kind as she talked through the upcoming show. The Kingdom Keepers were to be introduced to the passengers during the festive send-off, when the ship set out to sea. A mix of iconic Disney characters were set to entertain. Charlene felt uncomfortable spying on the meeting. But given the recent threats to Finn and Maybeck, the Keepers wanted to understand every detail of the show before going onstage. She listened intently when the leader described the onstage switch that would be made between the real Finn and his DHI hologram. It was a complicated maneuver that would come during a sword fight with a Cast Member playing Jack Sparrow.

"If something bad is going to happen, it's going to happen during the sword fight," Charlene told the Keepers thirty minutes later. The Sail-Away show was quickly approaching. "We should expect surprises."

"We should pay attention to the piece of fabric I found," Maybeck said. He had been hammering the group since the meeting had started. "Maleficent is aboard this ship. I have a piece of her robe to prove it. Jack Sparrow is way down the food chain in terms of magical powers. What's that? Oh, that's right," he snapped sarcastically, "he has none. Zero. But Green Nose? Name a power and she has it. She can literally be a 'fly on the wall' listening in to our conversations." Every Keeper suddenly looked around the small room. "Got your attention now, do I?"

Philby answered. "Maybeck, the discovery is great. Important. If she is here, then the journal is here. That's all that matters, all we're after. But listen, if the Overtakers are planning to kill Finn, by having Sparrow attack the real Finn instead of his DHI, we can prevent that from happening. The OTs will need to interfere with the ship's projection server. But we have an answer for that. One of Wayne's people installed a backup DHI server exactly for a moment like this. I can make sure

Finn's DHI appears onstage and stays onstage. Instead of killing Finn, that will kill their plan."

"Are you saying Wayne has other people working for him on the ship?" Charlene asked. "Does that mean he no longer trusts us to get stuff done for him?"

"I doubt that," Finn said.

"Because?" Charlene said.

Finn didn't have an answer.

"Yeah," she said, "that's what I thought." The Sail-Away Celebration was intended to be magical and memorable. As the first show of the cruise, it set a standard that told passengers, "This will be an amazing few days!" Cast Members smiled and ran around full of energy. Animation characters danced onstage beneath the gigantic Funnel Vision outdoor movie screen.

A Cast Member host welcomed the passengers. Cheers followed. Many passengers were already dancing in place or singing along to the thumping music. Daisy and Donald hooked arms and spun. Goofy looked goofy. More and more people began filling the Deck 12 balcony areas. Deck 11 was nearly at capacity. Two Disney songs played in a row. Some of the passengers were already in pirate costumes. Some wore bathing suits. The smell of sunscreen wafted as a steady breeze blew, the result of the ship plowing through the waters.

All at once Finn heard the host announce, "Please

welcome your Disney Hosts Interactive!" He followed Charlene, Philby, Maybeck, and Willa onto the small stage. Applause erupted. It was a rock-star moment, something he and the Keepers had learned to adjust to.

"D-H-I," rose the chorus. Cameras flashed. Passengers called them out by name. The Keepers waved.

Overhead, the Funnel Vision screen showed images and video of the DHIs as park tour guides. Pictures of the Disney villains were intercut. Maleficent, Cruella De Vil, Jafar, and others. As rumors had surfaced of a behind-the-scenes struggle between Good and Evil Disney characters, Disney had made the choice to pretend it was a new park story line. Rather than deny the truth, they played it up as fiction. The plan had worked. The crowd booed and cheered the images on the Funnel Vision display. Below, onstage, the Keepers took their places as the animation characters waved and departed.

The host's amplified voice roared over the crowd. "Here we are, making our way out into the seven seas, and you all know what that means?"

"We're cruising!" a passenger shouted.

"We're stuck on this ship!" another called out.

"Am I in heaven?" a girl's voice cried.

"It means," said the host, "we are not alone!"

The crowd liked what they heard. They cheered.

"Please wave a big hello to our sister ship, the *Disney*

Magic, off the starboard side!" The host pointed. The crowd saw the ship just coming into view. "It's a rare treat to pass a sister ship. Please give a big Disney shout-out to her crew. And don't forget to look for someone special!"

The distraction allowed stagehands to drop four ropes from the superstructure that held the Funnel Vision screen.

The ship's horn startled as it played the opening notes of "When You Wish Upon a Star." The *Disney Magic* sounded its horn, completing the melody. Another huge roar, this time from passengers on both ships.

The theme music from *Pirates of the Caribbean* played as the Funnel Vision screen showed the *Black Pearl*. The crowd booed loudly. Suddenly a pirate jumped from atop the ship's smokestack and slid down a rope. He landed onstage. A tremendous cheer arose. Three more pirates followed down the ropes.

"Jack Sparrow!" a young boy called.

The pirate drew his sword and rushed Finn.

This was not the script Charlene had described to the Keepers. Philby ran off stage. He'd left his laptop with a sound engineer. It was the only way to save Finn.

Seeing the show go off-script quickly filled Charlene with panic. *Anything can happen now*, she thought. And all of it bad. The Keepers were always being attacked. It didn't seem fair. But then again, when did witches and sorcerers play fair? Still, Charlene was tired of being a victim. She wished that for once, she and the Keepers would have the upper hand. Maybe, just maybe, Philby using the backup computer server could do just that.

17

ON THE BRIDGE of the *Dream*, a different kind of problem arose for the captain. When two Disney ships passed at sea, Mickey, Minnie, and other iconic characters could only appear on one of the ships. The idea was simple: Passengers were not to see two of the same character.

But something had gone wrong.

"Uncle Bob" Heineman had clear eyes and a boyish voice. As head of ship security, the so-called Mickey Rule came under his department.

"Captain, we've had a double sighting," Bob said privately.

Captain Hoken Cederberg stiffened. "Not on my watch, we haven't."

"Afraid so. Christian says our Mickey was not scheduled," Bob said, referring to the *Dream*'s director of entertainment, Christian Boyle. "Whoever's parading around Deck Eleven is an impostor. If it is a passenger, then the costume must be confiscated. I mustered the crew. I have a dozen hands looking for the impostor."

"Find him or her. And when you do, I want to question the offender personally."

"Understood." Uncle Bob grimaced. It wasn't going to be easy to find one person out of several thousand.

18

SWISH! THE TIP of the sword missed Finn's throat by a fraction of an inch. Jack Sparrow's eyes were dark and utterly calm. He didn't seem the slightest bit fazed at the idea of slicing Finn's throat. Another swipe. Sparrow cut the bandanna around Dale's furry neck.

The crowd cheered, believing it all a part of the show.

Following the script, two Cast Members arrived onstage to screen the real Finn as his DHI was to be projected. This was the moment for Finn to slip offstage. He tried. But something—someone—was holding him by the ankles. He looked down to see it was one of Sparrow's pirates. Another swing of the sword sliced the air with a hiss. Finn nearly lost an ear.

One of the Cast Members stepped forward to challenge Sparrow. The Cast Member's plastic sword was cut in two.

The crowd went wild. "Go, Jack!" "Get him, Finn!"

Finn twisted to break the grip on his ankle, but he lost his balance and fell to the stage. A grinning Jack

Sparrow stepped forward, ready to plunge his sword into Finn's chest.

With the tip of Sparrow's sword inches from Finn, the pirate was hit from the side. Sparrow went down hard. He lost his sword.

"Dill?" Finn said, utterly confused to see his neighbor and best friend. For it had been Dillard who had tackled Sparrow.

"Later," Dillard said. "Let's get you gone!"

As Dillard dragged Finn offstage, Jack Sparrow came to his feet, a knife in hand.

Sparrow rushed toward the side of the stage as Finn stepped back out onto it.

Jack Sparrow stabbed Finn in the chest.

A hush swept over the crowd. Only the lonely cry of a seagull was heard.

Finn's DHI stepped *through* Sparrow, raised his arms, and shouted, "Enjoying the show?"

The crowd hollered. Four Cast Members grabbed hold of the surprised Jack Sparrow and pulled him out of sight.

Sitting in sound booth in front of his laptop, Philby hung his head in relief. Finn's DHI showed on the screen. Philby had clicked the prerecorded script line, "Enjoying the show?" Of all the lines for him to put into the DHI's mouth, it seemed the best choice.

"Thanks, Philby," a shaken Finn said over his friend's shoulder. "Now maybe get my DHI offstage and end this thing."

"I'm on it," Philby said, working his trackpad. "Who was that kid that saved you?"

Finn spun around, searching for Dillard. He'd almost forgotten about that moment in all the confusion.

Before Finn could answer, a shrill voice rang out from the loudspeakers.

Chills rippled down Finn's back. He knew that voice.

19

SEEN ON THE Funnel Vision screen, Maleficent's head was the size of an SUV.

"And a villainous day to you all!" she said in her gravelly voice.

The crowd, still believing this to be part of the show, was dizzy with excitement. Their shouts of approval momentarily drowned out the dark fairy.

"Your so-called hero—I like to think of the boy as little more than a pest—has been taken care of, I trust?"

It was immediately apparent that Maleficent's address had been prerecorded. Finn had not been slain as she suggested.

"And you there!" Her green finger pointed. "You, in the booth. Don't bother trying to interrupt me. I'll stop when I feel like stopping."

She rocked her head. "You people with your practiced smiles and childish behavior. Listen to me. And listen well. Looking forward to the cruise, are you?"

Some in the crowd looked shocked by what they'd heard. Others, who weren't paying strict attention, raised their voices in support of enjoying themselves.

"Well, I wouldn't if I were you," said Maleficent. "Not with fairies like me around. Witches. Villains. Pick your poison." She cackled. "Poison! Now there's an idea." Her eyelids fluttered. They were the same vile green as the rest of her. "You might ask, 'What does she want?' but you'd be missing the point."

The screen went black, flickered, then returned to her image.

"The point is, you're mine," she said. "All mine! You won't reach land for another twenty-four hours. And even then, who says it will be safe for you? There is work to be done. Dark magic to employ." The blue sky overhead crackled with thunder. The crowd all ducked. Children cried out and rushed to their mothers, who held them tightly.

"Use your imagination," Maleficent said. "This is going to be fun." She waved her hand. Her image vanished. Only her voice remained. "At least for me."

20

FINN REREAD THE simple message on his Wave Phone. Whoever had sent him the text, whatever this was about, it had to end quickly. His mother had given him an eleven o'clock curfew.

People were just leaving the Buena Vista Theatre as Finn arrived. He didn't want to cause a fan moment, so he turned to the large windows looking out on the dark sea. Only a sliver of the moon hung in the sky, meaning the New Moon would offer the darkest night of the month within a day or two.

Right when we're on Castaway Cay, he thought.

His nerves jangled. The unexpected invitation on his phone continued to trouble him. How had someone gotten his number? Why was the message not signed? Why so mysterious?

He didn't want another encounter with Jack Sparrow.

At last, he entered what looked like an empty theater. His eyes adjusted to the dark.

Not empty, after all. He saw the back of a head

that faced an empty movie screen. Dark hair. Middle of a row.

Finn approached tentatively. Popcorn had spilled onto the carpet.

The girl pulled down the seat next to her without saying anything.

He inched his way down the row cautiously. She had dark hair dyed red at the tips.

"What you need to know," she said, "is that they're going to conduct a night test of two of the ship's lifeboats when we dock at Castaway Cay. Lifeboat numbers fifty-seven and twelve. You'll need to remember that."

"Who are you?"

"A friend."

"And I'm supposed to believe that?" Finn said.

"Believe what you want. I've never heard of a lifeboat test at night. Never mind the moment we dock. There's too much other stuff for the crew to be doing. I mean, do they test the lifeboats? Sure. All the time. But testing a lifeboat in the dark doesn't make any sense. The whole idea is they look for problems in or on the lifeboat. So, why do it in the dark?"

"Why are you telling me this?"

"They want you to know. They told me to keep my eyes and ears open for anything unusual. Well, this is unusual."

"They?"

"If you don't know who I'm talking about, then you're not as smart as everyone says."

"You don't have to be rude." Finn twisted in the seat. "A Cast Member, an impostor, tried to kill me today. Then he just disappeared. No one saw him after he'd been dragged offstage. So, maybe I don't feel like believing everyone I talk to."

"I have no control over entertainment. Boats fifty-seven and twelve. Memorize those numbers."

The door opened behind them. Pale light shone in.

The girl leaned over, put her hands on either side of his face, and kissed him. A serious kiss. A kiss he wasn't about to forget. She hugged him and whispered into his ear. "Play along. We're making out where we won't be seen."

"What?"

A flashlight beam hit them.

"Hello, there?" A man's voice. He sounded amused.

The fog in Finn's head cleared. The girl was inventing a reason for them to be hiding in the dark. He couldn't catch his breath.

She released Finn and leaned back in her own seat. "Hi," she said to the man.

"The theater is closed. You kids will have to find somewhere else."

"Please," the girl said. "Do we have to leave?"

"Afraid so," said the man.

"No problem," Finn said. He and the girl stood. She made a point of taking Finn's hand. They walked out like that as they passed the man.

"Please understand," she said quietly to Finn as they reached the passageway. "Whatever is going on, it means something."

Finn nodded. He still hadn't caught his breath.

"Find out what's going on with those lifeboats," she said. She nudged him toward the stairs.

Finn stumbled a few steps before recovering.

21

LATER THAT SAME NIGHT, Willa and Finn arrived as DHI holograms at the entrance to the Enchanted Garden restaurant. With no sign of Maleficent in the food storage area of Deck 2, the next place to look for the chilly fairy was the refrigerator section of the ship's central galley. Using the backup server in the Radio Studio, Philby had crossed them over into the ship's lobby.

"If we're caught," Finn said, reminding Willa, "we make sure they don't touch us—because of our holograms—and we say we're just trying to sneak a midnight snack."

"Perfect," Willa said.

Walking through the empty, darkened Royal Palace restaurant reminded Finn of being in the parks after dark.

At the far end, a set of doors led into the galley.

Waiters and waitresses carrying heavy trays used one set of doors to enter the restaurant and the other to return to the galley. Without speaking, and trying not to make a sound, Finn and Willa entered a large room filled with stainless steel. The place was squeaky-clean. All the pots, pans, utensils, and plates were stowed to avoid breakage as the ship rolled. The galley floor plan was divided by task: salad preparation, main dishes with stoves or grills. Glass-door refrigerators lined up like soda machines. There were a few night-lights, but the space was gloomy.

"It's like *Alice in Wonderland*," Willa said, "where she shrinks and everything's bigger." Everything in the galley was oversize.

Without speaking, Finn motioned to a large door in the wall with a thick, heavy handle. Lights and a digital thermometer put the internal temperature at 4.4 degrees Celsius.

Willa held up four fingers and then made an O with her thumb and index finger: forty. She had done the conversion to Fahrenheit. Cold, Finn thought, but not freezing. Perfect for Maleficent's resting place.

Finn reached for the handle to the walk-in refrigerator. Willa whispered his name. He looked up.

A creature more than seven feet high moved toward them. It had the appearance of a snowman, three white balls from floor to head. But the body was squishy, not ice crystals. It held a butcher's cleaver in its spongy hand.

"What is that?" a frightened Willa asked.

"It's the Fizzberry doughboy on steroids." Finn's voice quavered. "I don't think he wants us searching the walk-in refrigerator."

"Point taken," Willa said. "Can we go now?"

Finn glanced over his shoulder to the galley's second set of doors. "Maybe not."

A second faceless doughboy was coming toward them. This one was armed with a grill fork—two pointy tines on the end of a two-foot handle.

Finn swept his hologram hand through a work-bench. "The projections are good. We're going to be all right."

"I realize our holograms can walk right through them," Willa said. "But you first."

Knowing that fear could spoil his hologram, could make him partially human and therefore vulnerable, Finn didn't trust his ability to walk through a seven-foot monster made of bread dough. That could be a little scary. He handed Willa a metal baking rack. He said, "If we lead with these, we should be able to knock one of them out of the way and reach the doors."

"Two steps and the other guy will be on top of us," she said. "Bad idea."

"So, we each take one of them."

"Agreed," said Willa. "I've got Mr. Fork."

He and Willa turned back-to-back.

"Charge!" Willa said.

They rushed the doughboys, shoving a baking rack into the belly of each doughboy.

Neither monster moved an inch.

Instead, the white gooey dough absorbed the metal racks. The spongy flesh surrounded the racks like quicksand and sucked them into the center of the ball.

"Ewww!" Willa said, stepping back. "That is—"

"Disgusting!" Finn called out.

"So much for pushing them out of the way," she said. "And, note to self, mine looks really mad."

Finn's doughboy swung the meat cleaver, trying to separate Finn's neck from his shoulders. Finn ducked, but as he did, he felt a tingling shiver head to toe. He'd lost at least some of his hologram to fear. If the blade caught him, he would be cut. "Lost All Clear," he told Willa, meaning he was no longer pure hologram.

"Same," she returned, her back still to Finn. "Pardon the pun, but we're cooked." Willa cried out as she was stabbed in the shoulder with the grill fork. To her relief it passed through her hologram. She didn't feel any pain, didn't experience fear as Finn had.

"I seem to still be All Clear," she told him. *Pure hologram.* They both backed up to where they touched shoulder blades again. "Any ideas?"

"If you're All Clear," Finn said, "then get out of here while you can."

"And leave you?"

"Go get me some backup. I'll be fine."

"Sure you will," Willa said.

"You know that's the right call. If you lose your hologram, then we're both stuck in here. How much sense does that make?" Finn said.

"Olive oil."

"I don't think this is the time to discuss recipes."

"Trust me. My mother bakes a lot. You always put oil on dough because it makes it less sticky." Willa sounded so confident.

"Lowest shelf to your right," Finn said.

"Got it!" Willa spotted the gallon jugs of cooking oil.

"We need a match," she said.

"Because?"

She was losing patience with Finn. "Because if we turn them to crust they won't move."

The doughboys continued advancing.

Finn grabbed two jugs of oil. He handed one to Willa, twisting off its cap. He stepped forward, dodged another swipe of the butcher's cleaver, and spilled oil down the monster's front. Only a small amount spilled out. Then he allowed his imagination to take over. He planted the bottom of the jug into the doughboy's body. The dough absorbed the jug, just as it had the baking rack. As it sucked the jug into its belly, the oil spilled out, sloshing over its legs and onto the floor.

Willa copied Finn's technique. Soon oil was covering the fork doughboy.

Finn's doughboy took a step, slipped, and fell.

Willa's monster grabbed her shoulder. Seeing this, Finn picked up the fallen meat cleaver and sliced off the creature's arm. The wounded doughboy didn't scream, but bubbles of dough popped out of its mouth.

Willa took Finn by the hand and pulled him over to a workbench toward the stoves. "We need a match!" she said.

Finn knocked over a container of dry spaghetti. Its contents went everywhere. He picked up a single strand of spaghetti and used the stove to light its end. It caught flame like a match.

Willa stole it from him. She cupped the flame, slid back over the workbench, and set the oil on fire.

At first, the yellow flame spread slowly. Finn's fallen doughboy, struggling to sit up in the pool of slick oil, watched as the flames reached its feet. Its dough turned brown and blistered as the flame traveled. It turned from dough to crust, exactly as Willa had predicted. Its legs stiffened. Its belly boiled.

The air filled with the delicious smell of fresh bread.

Their shoes slippery with oil, the DHIs carefully hurried out of the galley and into the empty restaurant. From there, into the lobby. Finally, to the elevators.

The elevator car arrived. They stepped inside. The doors closed.

Finn sent Philby a text over his Wave Phone. His hands were shaking. "Why didn't I think of this back there?" he said.

"We were a little busy."

His message was one word:

Return!

When the elevator opened onto Deck 11, the car was empty.

22

FINN HAD SLEPT only two hours when his Wave Phone buzzed on the side table.

Lifeboats port side

He dressed quickly and snuck out of the suite. The girl with the red-tipped hair had been right.

Finn, Will, Charlene, and Maybeck met inside the forward running track tunnel on Deck 4. They had a commanding view of the port side lifeboats. Sure enough, there was activity as crew members readied two of the lifeboats. Philby stayed behind as a lookout, ready to warn the others over their Wave Phones.

The crew came and went as they worked. They fetched equipment, lines, and buckets. During one of the gaps when the deck was empty Finn said, "Charlene and I will take boat fifty-seven. You and Willa," Finn told Maybeck, "will find boat twelve."

"And then what?" Maybeck asked.

"We stow away," Finn said. "There's a cabinet in the bow where they keep life vests and stuff. Philby says it can hold two of us. Once in there, we listen for what's going on."

"That sounds easy," Charlene said.

"Yeah," Finn said. "That's what worries me."

They split up into teams, port and starboard—left and right. In pairs they hurried down the row of lifeboats suspended above the deck on either side of the ship.

Maybeck's artist eye caught sight of a pair of animal paw prints on the surface of the deck. He pulled out his Wave Phone to warn the others, all the while thinking: *There are no animals on this ship.*

He was too late.

"Are those hyenas?" Finn said, leaning his back against the wall.

Four mangy animals came toward him and Charlene. Their ribs showed beneath gray matted hair. The hyena telltale hump of shoulder and long neck separated them from being mistaken for dogs. Their pink tongues hung low, drool cascading down onto the deck.

"*The Lion King,*" Charlene whispered. "You remember how they—"

"I remember," Finn said. "They tear their prey apart, piece by piece. I pray we aren't their prey."

"Ha, ha," Charlene sniped. "Not exactly the best time for a joke, Finn."

Finn patted the pocket of his shorts. He withdrew a candy bar. "Okay," he said. "Here's the plan."

23

THE SHIP'S DECK shuddered as the captain's final maneuver pushed it to the pier on Castaway Cay. Crew members on the ship cast lines to those on the pier as the ship was secured. Far to the east, the black of the night sky transitioned to a rich blue. The sun would rise within the hour.

"Are those hyenas?" Willa asked Maybeck.

"I prefer mine barbecued," said Maybeck.

Two hyenas sniffed their way toward them.

"They're hunters, you know. They work in packs."

"And I need to know that because why?" Maybeck said.

"On that show, *Rogue Wild*, they capture alligators with those wire things. Like a noose."

"A neck snare," Maybeck said. "So?" He paused. "If you think I'm signing up to wrestle a hyena, forget it."

"Take off your belt."

"Say, what?"

She unfastened her belt and slipped it off. Her shorts sagged. "Do it now, slowpoke. Belt! Quickly!"

The hyenas closed in. Drool splattered the deck.

"They've picked up our scent," Maybeck said as he handed her his belt. "You are one weird girl."

Willa grunted as she grabbed a shuffleboard cue from a rack on the wall. She passed Maybeck a cue and a black disk. She kept one of each for herself.

"Awkward time for a game of shuffleboard, don't you think?" Maybeck said. "How about a rain check?"

The cue, a long pole to shove the shuffleboard disk down the deck ended in a semicircular Y. The Y cupped the disk for easier pushing. Willa tied the tongue end of her belt to the end of the cue. The buckle end formed a loop of leather.

"No way," Maybeck said, immediately copying her. "You really are a nerd."

"I prefer brainiac, but compliment accepted," Willa said.

"You and Philby are meant for each other."

"Eww," Willa groaned. "That's just wrong." She said, "We'll use the disks as bait. Loop goes around the disk. When they drop their nose to sniff the disk—"

"Yeah, I got it. I'm not a moron, you know."

"Could have fooled me," Willa said.

"Okay, Einstein," he said. "How does any of this

get us any closer to finding the journal? I mean, what's the point?"

"The point is that Wayne told a girl to tell Finn to check out the boats. If Wayne thinks it's important, then it is important."

24

Finn tossed a piece of the candy bar. The hyena charged, skidded to a stop, and snapped it up in one swipe of the long tongue. It swung its ratty head back and swallowed, its jaundiced eye fixed on Finn. *More,* the eye said.

Finn broke off another chunk and tossed it. With the hyena distracted, he and Charlene inched closer to a ladder leading to the lifeboats.

Charlene climbed like a spider. Finn scrambled up the ladder behind her. They slipped across a narrow catwalk to a lifeboat marked 57.

The fiberglass lifeboat had an arched roof so the boat could roll in the waves without taking on seawater. The boat looked like a plastic Easter egg lying on its side.

Finn extended his leg to reach the boat from the catwalk.

"Sit!" a woman's voice called out.

It wasn't Maleficent. Her voice was often low and manly, gravelly, and loathsome. But whoever it was, she sounded familiar to Finn. A Disney witch, or at least a character for certain.

Finn slipped inside the lifeboat. Charlene followed.

25

CONTROL! MAYBECK THOUGHT.

Wearing a belt around its neck, the hyena clapped its teeth loudly and squealed, having bit its own tongue. Maybeck held tightly to the shuffleboard cue that had lassoed the hyena's head. Willa caught hers only a moment later. Together, they dragged the hyenas to where Maybeck stuck his cue through the belt looped around Willa's hyena.

"We let go on three," Maybeck said, "and we run for the ladder up to the boats."

"With you," Willa said.

Maybeck counted down. They let go. Maybeck's cue being stuck through the neck loop meant the hyenas were tied together. When either moved it tugged the other. Neither liked this. They tore into each other, fangs showing.

Moments later, as crew members arrived, distracted by a rabid hyena fight, Maybeck and Willa slipped inside lifeboat number twelve. They crawled toward the front compartment and squeezed inside.

26

FINN TOOK NOTE of how little the crew spoke. Instead, the hum of the motor and the splash of water filled his ears. The air was close in the forward hold. It salted his tongue. He felt strange not knowing where the boat was taking him. Around in circles? Out to sea? *How does one test a lifeboat?* he wondered. He and Charlene sat pressed shoulder to shoulder, knee to knee. He could feel her heavy breathing against his rib cage. She was as scared as he was.

It occurred to him: He always knew where he was going. His parents drove him places. He rode his bike with a particular destination in mind. Being tucked into the pitch-black hold reminded him of waking up at night in the back of the car on a family trip. Only then had he wondered, *Where am I?* Like then, he had no answer. Charlene reached over and took his hand. Finn allowed it. Welcomed it. With tension seizing his body, a small comfort was all he could ask for.

The lifeboat jerked as the engine slowed.

"Anchor!" called a gruff voice.

We're inside the reef, Finn thought, the sound of

waves more present. The rise and the fall of the lifeboat became more apparent. So, they had been headed to shore from the start. Somewhere on the island. Why anchor a lifeboat if you're testing it? The girl had been right. Wayne had been right. These people were up to something.

Charlene moved Finn's hand to touch cold metal. It felt rough. Maybe shaped like a mushroom.

The anchor!

She pushed him past it, into the wedge of the pointed hull. They burrowed into a pile of life vests like badgers down a rat hole. Moving the vests to cover themselves, they held them in place as the small door opened.

A man's hairy arm reached inside, feeling for the anchor. Through the pile of vests Finn saw a shoulder and the top of a bald head. A clanging and a volley of swearwords rang out as the crewman freed the anchor. The rattle of a chain. The clap of a line.

But not the sound of the door closing.

"He left it open," Finn whispered. He adjusted one of the life vests to see more clearly.

Charlene grabbed his shirt and stopped him from going too far. Together they listened as a second, louder motor approached. The second lifeboat. Number twelve. Hopefully Maybeck and Willa were aboard.

The engine of their lifeboat settled to an idle. The boat shuddered and the engine stopped.

Finn and Charlene remained perfectly still.

A man's voice. "Quickly. We need that Creole freak back on board before sunrise."

Creole freak? Finn wondered.

A loud plop signaled the second lifeboat anchoring. Moments later, only the sound of voices and waves.

Finn edged forward, Charlene still holding his shirt. Their boat was empty.

Finn crawled carefully—silently—out the small door. He moved to the open exit in the lifeboat's hard-shell cover. He stole a look toward the beach, ten yards away.

Six men, the legs of their coveralls wet from the knees down.

Charlene arrived alongside Finn. "We're at the bungalows," she said.

"The which?"

"Like a spa on the beach. It's on the adult-only end of the island."

"You've been here before," Finn said.

"My mom loves Disney cruises."

"My first time," he said.

"Why here?" Charlene wondered aloud.

"The freaky Cajun," Finn said.

"Yeah, I heard that, too. Whoever that is."

"Psst!"

The tops of Maybeck's and Willa's heads showed from the hatch of the second lifeboat.

Finn motioned to the beach. Maybeck nodded. The four Keepers slid down fully into the water and swam slowly and quietly to shore.

Dripping wet, they crouched down on the beach and moved toward the row of small bungalows. Only one was lit from inside. The sky was tinged a brighter blue. Sunrise was nearly upon them.

Voices emanated from the lighted bungalow, a small, thatched shoe box of a cabin on three-foot stilts with wooden shutters across open-hole windows. Maybeck hand-signaled for the four of them to surround the bungalow, but to stay back. Finn returned two thumbs up. He remained by the wooden steps that led to the bungalow's only door. Maybeck and Willa went right, Charlene to the left.

Finn edged closer. The voices inside became clearer.

"You must come with us now." It was the gruff voice of the crewman from their lifeboat.

"You, I tell one more time," came a woman's low voice, spoken in a thick Jamaican accent. "I ain't going nowheres, mon. Ain't leavin' dis island till necessary. 'Tis them a-bringing it here to me, or it ain't happen no ways."

"Orders is orders," the man said.

"Ain't no matter to me. Them there be your orders, mon, not mine."

"Before sunrise, we were told," spoke the gruff man.

"Is you wishing to cross me, mon?"

"No, ma'am!" The gruff man sounded frightened. "If you choose not to come with us, then that's on you."

"'Tis on me, then," she said.

"You're not making my life any easier," said the crewman.

The woman said, "No life easy, mon."

"Have it your way," he said.

"That there's generally how it be done," she said with a chuckle.

Footsteps. The men were leaving.

Finn saw Charlene flatten into the sand by the next bungalow. Finn had nowhere to go but under the structure. He scurried past a set of the stilts and lay down in the soft sand.

The men muttered as they banged down the steps. One of them cursed the "old witch." Too loudly, apparently. For he made it only a matter of a few feet toward the water before he buckled in pain and fell to his knees.

"Names are what names is," came the woman's voice. She was standing in the bungalow's open doorway. "Best choose one's words carefully. Respect where respect be due." The weakened sailor was dragged by the others toward the boats. They moved quickly, like children eacaping from a ghost. Dark magic, Finn thought. He got away from the bungalow as quickly as possible. The others joined him amid a stand of palms trees.

"You know who that is in there?" Charlene whispered breathlessly. No one answered. "Tia Dalma," she said. "The voodoo priestess from *Pirates*."

For Finn, making that connection was like fitting a piece of a jigsaw puzzle into place. He nodded slightly. Swallowed dryly.

"They're taking the boats," Maybeck said. The lifeboat motors were groaning. "There goes our ride."

Finn glanced toward the ship tied to the pier. It seemed a long way off.

He saw the headlights of equipment and a dozen workers busy on the pier.

"Well, the dock is out," he said. "No way we are sneaking past all that." He pointed.

"We might be seen if we walk the beach," Willa said. "But we could get in the water with only our heads sticking out and get to the ship, I'll bet."

"So, we stay close to shore and just our heads out," Charlene said, "I like that."

The three looked to Finn for the final decision. It was always like this. He lived with weight on his shoulders. Wayne had once told him he would grow up to be the leader of the Keepers. Finn had never asked for that role. But he seemed stuck with it.

"We stay close," Finn said. He recalled his experience at Typhoon Lagoon—the last time he'd been swimming. "No one gets out front. No one lags behind."

The four moved as a group with only their heads above the waterline. After several minutes, light from the busy pier stretched to reach them. A flash, a silver shimmer, caught his eye. It appeared out in the deeper water.

"Hold up," he whispered. The Keepers bunched together.

"What is it?" Charlene asked.

Finn lowered underwater and opened his eyes.

A battery of barracuda was swimming directly into them.

"Don't move!" Finn said, easing his head above the water. "Don't breathe if you can. We have visitors."

A spinning swirl surrounded them. The school of barracuda thrashed the water into a foam. The fish were thin and very long. Each looked like a silver spear.

Finn spoke above the sound of the churning water. "They react to movement. Be still."

The barracuda continued to encircle the four

Keepers. Willa twitched and exhaled as a fish brushed her thigh.

The circle was closing.

Maybeck said, "I think they smell us, if that's possible."

"Ick!" Charlene cried out as the spinning circle of slimy fish rubbed against her legs. "I can't just stand here!"

"Ditto," said Willa.

"No kidding," echoed Maybeck.

Finn spoke calmly. "Okay. Slowly, gracefully, lie back into the water, chest out, arms out at your side."

"Isn't that called the dead man's float?" Charlene asked. "As in, dead man?"

"Do it now, please," Finn replied. He helped Charlene into a float. "Better?" he asked.

"Much," she answered.

Willa helped Maybeck and then adopted a floating posture herself. The hundreds of fish were inches away from their outthrust arms but no longer brushing their legs.

"Good call," Maybeck said.

"Can't stay here forever," Charlene said.

"I'm on it," Finn said. "Take deep breaths and hold it. You float higher."

"Finn!" Charlene called out.

He disappeared underwater.

Finn had been thinking hard about Typhoon Lagoon. Of Triton holding back Ursula, of Amanda holding back the wave. He'd been trying to remember the code Triton had offered. *Something to do with starfish. Fly? High? Cry?* Then he had it!

The barracuda, startled by the three Keepers lying back into a float, now closed in from all sides. Finn saw this through blurry open eyes, his head fully underwater.

"Starfish wise, starfish cries." The words bubbled out of his submerged mouth. He tried again, shouting louder. More bubbles. Nothing close to words. All a mumbled nonsense.

Nothing changed. If anything, the barracuda were tightening the circle.

Finn resurfaced, gulping for air.

The turbulent water crushed in on the four Keepers. Finn could feel sharp teeth scratching his legs.

"Ow! I just got bit on my finger! I'm freaking out here," Maybeck announced.

Willa, remaining surprisingly calm in her float, lifted her hand just high enough to point in the direction she was looking. "Finn!"

He turned his head ever so slowly. There were a thousand flying fish careening toward them. As the school reached the ring of froth, it disappeared. Triton's code had failed. "Come back!" Finn whispered.

All at once, seawater erupted between the Keepers and the barracuda. A circular wall of flying fish rose like a fountain several feet tall. For a few seconds the water whipped into a tumult. The ring of suds beyond the fountain of flying fish subsided. The waters calmed. The fountain of fish stopped in an instant. The airborne fish flipped and tumbled into the water and were gone.

The Keepers took several long minutes to recover. Maybeck said he might have spoiled his pants. Everyone but he laughed. His finger was bleeding badly. They swam back to the ship, steering clear of the activity on the pier. Finding an open loading area with stairs leading from the two empty lifeboats, the Keepers sneaked back aboard. They split up, taking different elevator banks and different stairs to their staterooms.

Finn wondered how any of what they'd seen and heard in the bungalows might have something to do with the missing journal. He couldn't figure it out. He kept thinking of the state-fair booth where he'd watched a coffee bean be hidden under one of three shells. The shells were then shuffled around quickly. He had to guess which shell hid the bean. No matter how many times he watched the hands move the shells, Finn couldn't get it right. He lost.

How much of what was going on—the attack at the Sail Away, in the galley, the bungalows—involved the journal, and how much of it was just moving shells around as some kind of trick?

27

THE NEXT MORNING, the Keepers met the ship's entertainment crew in a forward lounge called Pink. They were there with Minnie, Mickey, Chip, and Dale, and others scheduled for Castaway Cay meet and greets.

The Keepers needed a good number of questions answered. Why was Tia Dalma on Castaway Cay? Why had the crew tried to take her aboard the *Dream*? Did Tia Dalma have something to do with the journal?

When the time came to leave the ship for the island, Willa and Charlene followed two Cast Members, both girls. Overheard whispering to each other, one had said, "What if we're caught?" The other had replied, "I'd rather lose my job than be turned into a frog for the rest of my life."

A dozen activities were already under way on the island. Swimming, Jet Skis, snorkeling, Castaway Ray's Stingray Adventure, waterslides, sailing. Children squealed with joy as their freshly oiled parents stretched out on *Disney Dream* beach towels.

By the light of day, the island revealed itself. A

mile-long white sand beach stretched along the shore. Mangroves and jungle scrub occupied most of the rest of the spit of land. Dirt and sand paths had been cut throughout, some from a hundred years earlier when the island had been a private plantation.

Keeping an eye on the two suspicious Cast Members from the back of a trolley shuttle, Charlene and Willa remained alert for anything unusual. When the girls climbed off the shuttle in the middle of an old runway, the Keepers followed.

The asphalt runway looked like a black ribbon dividing the jungle of palm trees and bushes. An old prop plane and some steamer trunks and luggage, overgrown by vegetation, aimed out at the strip.

As the shuttle stopped, Charlene climbed off and headed to explore the airplane. Willa got off and pretended to tie her sneakers. The shuttle pulled away. When Willa looked up, Charlene was no longer by the overgrown airplane. Willa hurried down the nearest path where the two Cast Members had gone. The trail was cut through prickly shrubbery. Ten yards ahead the trail divided.

A confused Willa stood there a moment before Charlene popped out of the jungle scrub and scared her half to death.

"They went to the right," Charlene said, pointing.

"What are they doing way out here?" Willa asked, her voice in a knot. "There's nothing but nothing."

"Our job is to find out."

"I've got a bad feeling about this," Charlene said. They moved down the path without talking. Whenever it curved, they took care to peer ahead so they didn't come across the two Cast Members. The bushes grew thicker. Twisted, dark branches looked like skeleton arms. The air of decay, of salt marsh and mud. After several minutes, Charlene reached out to block Willa. Voices could be heard not far away.

"The fireworks will hold everyone's attention." A boy's voice.

"No kidding," a girl said. "But what's with the black hose?"

"That's for later. Just do your jobs and collect the hose. If you're lucky enough to be there tonight, you'll see."

Willa and Charlene ducked into the dark mangrove. Something was being dragged. It was coming toward them.

They peered out of the thicket. The two Cast Members from the shuttle were hauling thick coils of black hose. So was a college-age boy, six feet tall and lifeguard-handsome. The hoses looked heavy and hard to carry. They carved snakelike patterns into the sandy path.

28

PEOPLE RARELY QUESTIONED Maybeck. Even adults. He knew no one would stop him as he passed a sign: CAST MEMBERS ONLY. Dressed in the Cast Member khaki shorts and pale blue polo, he walked down a rutted sand road. He was a person who belonged backstage. He was, in fact, a spy.

The presence of Tia Dalma suggested someone on the island staff must know that she was staying in a bungalow. But why shelter the Cajun queen?

The crew area was littered with all sorts of equipment. A miniature tractor, bicycles, and a dozen "Pargos"—golf carts converted into small trucks. There were rows of propane gas tanks for barbecues; stacks of wooden fence poles. The place looked like a rent-it center. Of the few outbuildings, a metal Quonset hut sheltered more equipment. Nearby, a white concrete building, its one window holding a groaning air conditioner, had a hand-painted sign over the door: HEADQUARTERS. A plank next to the door read, OUT OF MY MIND. BACK IN FIVE MINUTES.

Maybeck didn't knock. Not his way to do things. He

entered a small room. At the back were a pair of offices. In the far corner, a guy in his midtwenties was reading a book and drinking coffee. His name tag read "Tim." Maybeck nodded. Tim said hello, never lifting his head. Two bulletin boards held notices and alerts.

REMEMBER TO SHUT OFF ALL PROPANE VALVES
EVERY NIGHT!

FRESH WATER IS A LUXURY! CONSERVATION FIRST!

PERSONAL HYGIENE IS THE BEST AMBASSADOR—
REMEMBER TO SHOWER!

THERE'S A WAITING LIST TO WORK ON CASTAWAY.
EARN YOUR PLACE HERE.

Another note caught his eye:

TO WHOEVER IS MESSING WITH THE MARINE RADIO: STOP IT!

IT MUST BE LEFT SET TO RECEIVE DISTRESS SIGNALS.

BY RESETTING THE FREQUENCY, YOU ARE ENDANGERING LIVES!

The message seemed unusual to Maybeck. He memorized it. Philby might find it important.

"You're new," the guy in the corner said. He seemed

to have come awake. It wasn't a question, but a statement.

"Off the ship," Maybeck said. "Training. Bummer is, I don't get to stay."

"You look familiar."

"Yeah, I get that a lot. Mostly from the ladies."

The reader grinned. "I hope you get the gig."

"Everyone wants to work here."

"I was like that," the boy said. "But it can also be pretty boring at times."

"Not right now?" Maybeck said.

"No way. Super busy. They added the fireworks tonight. That's so cool for us. That never happens."

Maybeck took a mental note. *Something different.*

Presenting himself as indifferent and uncaring, inside Maybeck was much different. He had built a shell thick enough to take sideways glances. In school, Black kids were supposed to be athletes. He was an artist. Being handsome and tall, he was looked up to. He wanted none of that. Girls liked him and he liked them, but only as friends. He didn't feel like the smooth kid he pretended to be. Social situations made him uncomfortable. His defense was humor and feigned superiority. Everyone seemed to have a best friend. His was his aunt, Bess. Maybeck longed for the boy or girl whom he could trust with his fears and concerns. Someone to text with late at night. Someone who cared. Month by month, the other Keepers had become those kinds of friends for him. But none was a best friend. The guy in the chair probably had a best friend. Most kids did.

"What have they got you doing today?" the reader asked.

"Trash," Maybeck said without hesitation. He figured a trainee would start at the bottom.

"Figures."

"No kidding."

"My advice," the guy said, "put it in a second bag as you take it out of the can. The crabs get in the cans and when the bottom falls out of those bags it is beyond disgusting."

"Good to know," Maybeck said.

"You should be glad you got trash duty. I have to walk the hoses."

"Hoses?" Maybeck said.

"Mosquito control is a little different here. Eco-friendly. We pump carbon dioxide through a soaker hose that's treated with bug killer. The bugs are attracted to the gas. They land on the hose. Bam! End of the line. No more spraying from planes and stuff that poisons everything."

"Never heard of that. Pretty cool."

"Pressure in the hose has been fluctuating, which

usually means a leak. There must be ten miles of hose out there."

"Good luck with that," Maybeck said.

"Me? I think it's a waste of time to check them. Has to be another case of bad communication. Pressure goes down when a hose breaks. Sure it does. But fluctuate up and down? That's got to be somebody disconnecting it, repairing it, and putting it back together. Right? Otherwise, tell me how it makes any sense?"

Get a life, Maybeck wanted to say. But he didn't. This guy and his hoses. "I really couldn't say," he said for real.

"You like the ship?" He put down his book, grabbed an oversize hat, and followed Maybeck toward the door.

"Yeah, it's all right, I guess. Tight quarters. Long hours."

"Same at this place," said the guy who'd been reading. "See you out there." He left the compound, heading down a narrow path. He followed the black hose that connected to another of the outbuildings.

"See you," Maybeck said.

29

A SET OF BUOYS marked where guests could feed and pet stingrays. Finn touched the note in his pocket that he'd found wrapped into his fresh laundry bundle. It told him to be here at this exact time. Here he was.

Finn waded out toward the buoys, lifting his shorts to avoid getting wet. Focused as he was on his shorts, he didn't look up until he was halfway out.

The girl Cast Member with the red-tipped hair looked back at him. She appeared to be in charge of the stingray attraction.

"Pretend like I'm training you," she said as Finn reached her, "just in case anyone should ask."

"Got it," Finn said.

"Storey," she said.

"Which one?"

"My name. Storey Ming."

"Ah. I'm Finn."

"Duh," she said.

A plastic track ran just below the water's surface. The stingrays had been trained to swim the track. They stopped to be fed and petted. Storey Ming held some green pellets in her hand. A stingray stopped and hovered over her palm. She told Finn to pet the fish, which he did.

"Wild," he said.

"Your turn." She handed him pellets. He opened his hand in the center of the tray, exposing the pellets. The next stingray stopped and sucked the pellets away. It felt creepy, but also exciting.

"Whoa," he said.

"Yeah," Storey said, "we get that a lot."

"Why am I here?" he asked.

"You're supposed to tell me about the lifeboats."

"Am I?"

"Line opens in five minutes, Finn. It has got to be fast."

He looked to the shore, where guests were queued up waiting to wade in.

"Sure," he said.

"Better," she said.

He told her about the encounter with the hyenas, about stowing away on the lifeboats, and following the sailors to the bungalows. He mentioned hearing voices. He wasn't sure why, but he left out the part about Tia Dalma. Not everyone could handle the world of the Keepers and Overtakers. He didn't want to lose this girl. She was a valuable ally.

"And that's all?" she said. She sounded disappointed. Like being chased by hyenas was nothing. Like he didn't think her being right about the lifeboats was any big deal.

"I mean," Finn said, "you were right about the lifeboats. They weren't testing them."

"Then what?"

He had tripped himself up. How was he supposed to explain without lying? He sighed. "The guys in the lifeboats were there to pick up Tia Dalma. Only she wouldn't go. They argued. They wanted her on the *Dream*. She didn't budge."

Storey stared at him. Then toward the beach. "Tia Dalma is on Castaway? That's not right. Here they come. Quickly, Finn."

"Tia Dalma tied one of the sailor guys into knots. I mean, he fell down in pain, and all he'd done is call her a name."

"You're sure about that?" Storey asked.

"Is that a big deal?"

"You're asking me if it's a big deal that the real Tia Dalma is on Castaway Cay? A voodoo witch doctor? Some place she doesn't belong. Doesn't ever belong!"

"Well, if you put it that way," Finn said. "It seemed odd to me."

"Odd? It's unheard of. Why Tia Dalma?" Storey sounded terrified.

"There's this thing I can't tell you about," Finn said. "I'm sorry. But if it somehow connects to Tia Dalma then we have big problems. She can cast spells. I saw it."

"It's not fair sharing a secret that you don't share," Storey said. "That's just plain mean."

"I said I was sorry."

"Because the Kingdom Keepers are special," she said.

"Now who's being mean?" he said.

Storey signaled the Cast Member onshore. The guests began wading toward them.

Meeting over.

30

FINN'S MOTHER WAVED him over to a picnic table. The air smelled of bacon, barbecue, and sunscreen. Small waves rolled ashore as two-man sailboats glided past the outer buoys.

"I feel as if I've barely seen you," she said. She wore a short sundress over a one-piece bathing suit. Same as she always wore.

"Busy, you know," he said.

"You'd tell me if you were in any kind of trouble. Any kind of danger." She wore her worry on her forehead.

"Probably. Maybe not. But if you asked, I would." Finn tried to read her eyes through her sunglasses. *How much did she really want to know?*

"Well, aren't you the plucky one," she said with a baffled grin. "Is that a challenge?"

"Maybe a warning?" he said tentatively.

"Mrs. Philby can't get her son off his computer."

"We're all in trouble if she does."

"Okay. Good to know," his mother said. She lowered her sunglasses and looked out over the top of them. Her signal that she meant business.

"There's a character here on the island," Finn said. "She has powers, Mom. Big powers. She doesn't belong. Wayne tipped us off. Sort of. It got complicated. You know when you know something, but you can't figure out what you know? It's like that."

"A puzzle," she said, returning the glasses to hide her eyes.

"Yeah. Exactly."

"The trick to solving a puzzle is to not allow yourself to get overwhelmed. Like a jigsaw puzzle. You just focus on the one piece and let the bigger puzzle solve itself. Does that make sense?"

"Sort of, I guess," Finn said.

"Sometimes it's a matter of steps and not getting ahead of yourself."

"Uh-huh." *How would she feel about hyenas chasing him?*

"Me and the others—"

She interrupted. "The others and I."

"Whatever. We have this stuff to do as DHIs. You know, we are the first hologram characters on the ship, and all that. And then there's stuff for Wayne. The Overtakers. This thing we've got to find. We've got to get back. And there's this girl—"

"A girl?"

"Mom, not like that. Eww. No. Anyway, she's older than me."

"Than I. She's older than I."

"Mom! She knows stuff about all this. But I don't know if I can trust her. I mean, I want to. And so far, she hasn't lied. But the OTs don't play fair. So, there's that."

"Complicated," his mom said.

"You could say that."

"Looks as if she got him off the computer," she said, looking over Finn's shoulder.

Philby was approaching. Of all the Keepers he was the palest. His ginger complexion didn't help any.

"Hello, Dell," she said. "I'll leave you two." She gathered up a canvas bag. She whispered to her son, "You be careful. I'm here if you need me." Finn thanked her.

Philby sat down, his eyes on a honeybee as it buzzed past. It seemed out of place, so far from the mainland. It settled near a ketchup stain and then flew off. In his science class they had studied how when a hive was threatened, certain bees rushed to surround the queen and protect her. He wondered if that applied to Tia Dalma as well.

"Hey," he said.

"Hey," Finn said.

"You in trouble?" Philby asked.

"Nah. Everything's good. My mom says your mom is trying to get you off your laptop."

"I've been monitoring our backup server. So far, no one has discovered it on the LAN. I can cross you guys over whenever. When you're asleep, I mean. Same as always. Only on the ship. Not here on the island."

"Something is going down tonight," Finn said. "They added a fireworks show."

"Yeah. They'll be shot from the ship. But people can watch from the beach."

"Why would they add that?" Finn asked.

"Probably just because it's cool."

"But if it's not that?"

Philby was briefly lost in thought. "Tia Dalma can do voodoo. Like stick pins in dolls and stuff like that."

"What's that got to do with fireworks?"

"Nothing. I've been thinking about Maleficent. That video during the Sail Away. The journal. The incantation Wayne told you about. Chernabog. Especially, the hyenas. Maleficent or Tia Dalma could probably make the hyenas happen."

"So?" Finn said.

"Remember that dude, the secret agent guy in the museum? He told you something was being moved."

"So?" Finn said, repeating himself.

"I think it all ties together, Finn. The journal. What Wayne said. That message you got."

"How?"

"I need to get back to the ship without my mom seeing me," Philby said, thinking of the bees surrounding the queen. "I know we have to do stuff at lunch. That thing as tour guides. That maybe takes an hour, max. Before the fireworks happen we have to know what's going on. Something's going down."

"Tell me something I don't know," Finn said. He felt frustrated. He kept thinking in circles. Philby was rehashing the past. "Storey—the girl in the theater, her name is Storey—was freaked to hear Tia Dalma was here."

"Tia Dalma has witchcraft and abilities Maleficent does not. That voodoo stuff is nuts."

"And they wanted her on the ship," Finn said.

"Maybe they're going to try to get her again tonight," Philby said. "Maybe the fireworks are a distraction."

"We should keep an eye on the bungalow," Finn said.

"We should keep an eye on the bungalow," Philby echoed.

As Finn was leaving the dining area, he spotted Sally Ringwald alone at a table. He stopped, unable to move. There was no way she belonged here or on the cruise. It made no sense.

"What are you doing here?" Finn said too loudly.

"I'm not alone," she answered. "Luowski is on the ship. Others, too."

Finn thought about Dillard showing up during the Sail Away. "Your parents?"

She nodded. "Free offer was emailed to my mom."

"No way," he gasped.

"Same for all of us."

"All?"

"Yeah, well. It's not just Luowski and me."

The Overtakers had hacked the reservations system, Finn thought. Or they'd put someone under a spell to change things.

Sally cleared her throat. "I promised your mother."

"To spy," Finn said.

"Not so loud, you idiot."

Finn sat down. He felt punched in the gut. "Dillard?"

"Never heard of her."

"He's a him."

"No clue." Sally spoke softly. "There's something happening tonight."

Tell me something I don't know. "Such as?"

"A bunch of us are going to stay on the island for the fireworks."

"To do what?"

"Not sure. But it's not to watch the show. There's a truck involved. Luowski's part of it."

"Okay," he said. But it wasn't okay. Not at all.

"I thought you should know. It's something I thought you should know."

"You said, 'Part of it.' Part of what?" he asked. "Who, besides you guys? Maleficent?"

Sally stood from the bench. "I thought you should know, that's all."

Finn called out to her, but she walked away without looking back. It was only then he realized she was dressed as a Cast Member.

31

"Face it, we're lost," Charlene said. She and Willa had been arguing, blaming each other for having no idea where they were. It was hot and they were thirsty. They had been wandering the narrow trails for more than two hours. They needed to tell Finn and Philby about the Cast Members lugging sections of hoses. Maybe *stealing* the hose.

"Wait a second!" Willa said. "In the morning there's a land breeze. In the afternoon, it's a sea breeze. It's all about the sea heating the air early in the morning."

"Translation, please," Charlene said.

"Wind," Willa said. "If we move with the wind to our backs, we'll be heading for the water."

"We're on an island, Willa. We're surrounded by water."

"Exactly. It's perfect."

"I have no idea what you are talking about."

"What you said: it's an island. A small one. Once we hit water, we just start walking. At some point we circle around back to the beach."

"You mean we've been walking in circles for nothing," Charlene said.

Willa licked her finger and stuck it high in the air. She felt one side of it cool. "Follow me," she said.

32

A SEAGULL FLEW lazily above the beach on Castaway Cay. Below, preparations for the Beach Blanket Barbecue were under way.

A pink sun dipped below the horizon, swallowed by the Atlantic Ocean. Beach chairs were wiped down. Barbecue grills puffed delicious gray smoke. The volley-ball court was raked and ready. A hundred tiki torches were lit, their dancing yellow flames waving like small hands. *Come.*

A stream of freshly scrubbed passengers flowed from the *Dream.* In the distance, the music of steel drums beckoned. *Party time.*

The gull continued its uncharted path, riding the air currents, watching the waves lap to shore. Other men were uncoiling black hoses along the island's disused runway. Soft light flickered from one of the cabanas.

The gull did not have what humans think of as memory. But there were images floating around in its pea-size brain. Men and women busy within the jungle. Heightened activity within the Cast Member compound.

Somewhere within the gull came a single message: *Everything is different tonight.*

It was time to find a place to settle and sleep. Maybe by morning things would be back to normal.

33

SHUTTERS, THE CRUISE ship's photo shop, displayed hundreds of new pictures each evening. One passed through Shutter's Vista Gallery when walking aft on Deck 4. Finn headed in that direction to meet up with the rest of the Keepers before leaving the ship for the barbecue. He'd received a text that Willa, and Charlene had returned from getting lost on the island. He was eager to talk to them. His mind was on the girls' adventure as he moved through the gallery. He could imagine a dozen explanations of how they'd become lost. Including an encounter with Overtakers.

Finn stopped abruptly. He wasn't sure why he stopped, only that he had to. Something had triggered it. He looked around, wondering if he were being followed. No one. But hundreds of smiling faces, white-flashing teeth, faced him. Pictures of families, of couples with kids, beamed from flat-screen displays. The walls held printed photos as well. Most of the photos had been taken earlier on Castaway Cay. Others had been photographed in the dining rooms, or around the ship's pools. The faces were bright and happy. Suntanned and sand-sugared.

All but a few. The other faces had been caught in profile. The person being photographed had turned away. These few people were not smiling. Their jaws were set. Their eyes hidden behind sunglasses. Their expressions, determined. They did not want their pictures taken.

One was the face of Sally Ringwald. He'd seen her earlier. She had relayed the message that a truck was being prepared for some excursion or operation. *Something is going down tonight*, Finn recalled thinking.

No, it was another person in profile, not Sally, that had stopped Finn. Another person trying to hide from the cameras. But who? His eyes jumped from photo to photo, smile to smile. All the happiness on display was too much to take. There was trouble coming to the island. Trouble of which these pleased people knew nothing. Trouble that was the Keepers' job to discover and stop. A journal to be found and recovered.

There was the jaw in profile. The hard forehead. The slightly crooked nose from one too many punches. The red hair.

Greg Luowski.

Finn's head swam. Just as Sally had told him.

But there was no mistaking the bully. The camera didn't lie. Finn hurried to the counter and ordered a print of the photograph. A smiling couple holding an infant who wore a floppy blue hat. Behind, and between the infant's head and his father's, a boy with green eyes focused on the camera with pure hatred.

34

MAYBECK WALKED THE sand-covered asphalt track that led to the Cast Members' island maintenance area he had visited earlier. He hoped to find Tim, the guy who'd been reading. He hoped for an explanation. Willa and Charlene had witnessed Cast Members separating and gathering sections of the black soaker hose used for insect control. The Cast Members had lugged the coils of hose a great distance. If the girls hadn't become lost, they might have seen where the hose had ended up. Maybeck hoped that Tim knew.

The sun was still setting, the sky darkening. Shadows stretched thin. A window on the near side of the Quonset hut stood open. It had been closed earlier. Maybeck entered the small Cast Member hut where he'd first met Tim. The place was empty. It made sense given all the activity at the Beach Blanket Barbecue. Tim's book sat next to the chair, open and turned upside down on a small table.

"Hello? Tim? Anyone?" Maybeck called out. He shivered. It wasn't the air conditioning.

A shoelace. It stuck out from beneath the closet's closed door. A neon-orange shoelace.

Maybeck approached the closet door cautiously. The air conditioner behind him huffed and coughed and groaned.

He opened the closet door. Tim's face showed he had been roughed up by someone. His hands were tied, his mouth gagged. Maybeck quickly loosened the gag.

"Maintenance shed," Tim groaned as Maybeck worked to untie his hands. "It's bad. We were missing a couple propane tanks. The minute I mentioned it, this dude slugged me." Tim sat forward to untie his ankles. He cried out from a sharp pain.

"You stay. I've got this," Maybeck said. Overtakers didn't beat up kids. They might try to kill you, but that was different. This—what had been done to Tim—was the work of mere mortals.

Maybeck hurried to the Quonset hut's open window. Metal bars across the window prevented him from climbing in. He peered into the dark hut. There was a tractor and other large machinery. Immediately in front of him was a machine shop: a drill, a band saw, and a grinder. He could smell fresh paint and wondered if that was why the window was open.

Standing perfectly still, Maybeck heard faint sounds coming from inside. *A keyboard clicking?*

Maybeck snuck around front. He cracked open the door and put his eye to it. Slipped inside. Walked deeper into the hut. Across from the machine shop was a desk. Gear obstructed Maybeck's view. He knelt to get a better look.

He saw a hairy leg. It wore a black flip-flop. The leg lacked any kind of tan. Whoever it belonged to had not been on the island long.

Pale reddish skin. *Philby?*

Moving extremely carefully, Maybeck slipped past a tractor tire and obtained a better view. He could only see the person's back. A strong back. *Not Philby.* Maybeck waited. And waited. Finally, the person's head turned.

It was Greg Luowski.

35

THE MUSIC OF a wood xylophone, a bamboo flute, and a steel drum floated in the air. Finn crouched among the wide elephant-ear plants outside Tia Dalma's cabana. He was there to keep an eye on the Cajun queen. The shutter was open. Candlelight flickered through the open-air window. A shadow swept past on the sand. Finn crawled beneath the cabana. A rope was coiled around the cabana's stilt.

As Finn crouched the rope began *moving*. It uncoiled like a snake.

It *was* a snake.

The thing slithered into the sand toward Finn. It stopped. Half of it raised up like a stick. Its head fanned out.

A cobra!

Its eyes flashed red. They glowed hypnotically. It looked exactly like Jafar's staff.

Finn felt himself move. His knees skidded in the sand toward the snake. It had a grip on him both physically and mentally. He couldn't look away. The murmur of voices caught his attention. A man and a woman

were speaking. Jafar and Tia Dalma? Jafar's staff—
the snake—had been left out front to keep watch.

Finn fought to break eye contact, but the snake
had a hold on him. He struggled to scoop up some
sand. Dug his heels in. It was no use. He was being
pulled. The cobra's eyes grew larger, their effect more
powerful.

Using every ounce of his strength, Finn lifted his
arm. He threw the sand into the cobra's eyes. The snake's
eyes squinted shut. The spell broke.

Finn dove forward. He grabbed hold of the stick
section of the snake. The staff. He swung it against
the stilt.

The tail end wrapped around the stilt and pulled the
rest of it loose from Finn's hand. The cobra's flashing
tongue was suddenly an inch in front of Finn's face. Finn
fell back. The stick end softened into a snake's body.
Finn grabbed hold a second time. Without thinking, he
tied the snake into a knot around the stilt. It struggled
to unknot itself but was stuck.

Overhead, shouting could be heard. Both Tia Dalma
and Jafar were upset.

Finn put an eye to the cracks in the flooring. The
glimmer of candlelight revealed the cabana's thatched
roof. Finn heard more clearly through the floorboards.

". . . is unacceptable." Jafar's voice.

153

"All things given time," Tia Dalma said. "There is but the one cause."

"Promises were made."

"Not by me, they wasn't." Tia Dalma was losing patience.

"You know who I mean," he said.

"The green fairy does not break her promises."

"I am owed the lamp. My purpose in joining this journey is the fulfillment of years of effort. Any delays like this—"

"—must be important, eh? Trust, we must."

"I trust no one. Not my own shadow."

"Thems of us who want, want what you want. Perhaps they is for the different reasons. The hallow is important to every one of us."

"You conjure this and that," Jafar said. "It is more for you than for me."

"What is so very difficult, hmm?" Again, Tia Dalma sounded like she was in a hurry.

"Children! Gooey-eyed, wet-lipped little spoiled brats all begging for an autograph. It is an insult to my dignity."

"It is not so very difficult to wait. This, I think. Another some days. Then the hallow. Think of the power. Think of all that power."

Silence. A gruff chuckle. "Perhaps you are right."

"I am never anything but," said Tia Dalma, adding a chortle. "If I could lie, even with great difficulty, how much easier my existence. This is my curse. This is my legacy. So be it."

Another long silence. "Go in peace," Jafar said.

"And you."

The boards creaked. Sand rained onto Finn's head. He scurried out from beneath the cabana. Crossing the sand, he lay down flat in the shadow of the adjacent structure. He slowed his breathing.

"What have we here?" Jafar said, his voice incredibly close.

At first, Finn was convinced he'd been spotted. Thankfully, he was wrong.

"Got yourself tied in knots again?" Jafar said. "Do you never learn? Must I *what*? What's that?"

Finn had only seconds to try to understand. Jafar had to be talking to the snake. That meant the snake was talking to Jafar. That meant Jafar was being told of a boy under the cabana.

Jafar panicked. He poked his head under the cabana.

Finn rose to his feet, stayed low, and took off running.

"You!" Jafar called out.

Finn ran through the patches of moonlight. He weaved his way between the huts for cover. Without looking he sensed the cobra was coming for him. He was right. It darted alongside and struck at Finn's ankle. The boy jumped. The cobra missed.

Together, Finn and the cobra raced through picnic tables crowded with guests from the *Dream*. A man screamed. A woman called for her children. Trays of food spilled, raining down french fries and hamburger buns.

Finn never slowed. His legs struck and broke through some sort of plastic ribbon. He heard a boy's voice shout, "Heads up!"

A dart flew past Finn's right ear. He was inside a beach-dart competition. The errant dart hit the cobra in the head. The snake instantly turned to wood. Finn saw it happen but did not slow down. He hurdled the next length of tape. Now on open beach, he ran ever faster, desperate to put distance between himself and Jafar's walking stick.

36

For the third time, Willa tried to explain what she and Charlene had heard while they were in the mangroves. There had been mention of a plane. A box. A delivery. The hoses they carried. Combined, it seemed to tell a story. But it was not one that Philby understood.

"The fireworks will be starting soon," he said. They stood near Monstro Point, the whale digging site. Most of the activity was down the beach at Grouper and Gumbo Limbo.

"I think whatever this is, it's happening then," Willa said. "During the fireworks."

"Agreed. So, I'll watch the runway," Philby said. "I can hide by the old plane."

"I'll find Charlie," Willa said. "She can help Finn keep watch at the cabanas. Then I'll meet you at the old plane."

"Wait a second!" Philby said. "Isn't that Finn down there on the beach, running like his hair is on fire?"

37

Maybeck resisted the temptation of trying to sneak up on a kid like Luowski. The dude was big, strong, and angry most of the time. Challenging Luowski wasn't going to get Maybeck anywhere but in a whole lot of pain.

Instead, he kept watch.

At exactly nine thirty, moments before the fireworks were scheduled, Luowski slipped on a pair of headphones. He said, "Roger, King Air, Tango-Charlie-four-five-two-two. This is Sandbar. Come around to vector thirty."

Maybeck heard the first mortar launch, a deep, concussive blast. It signaled the start of the fireworks. A moment later, colorful light flashed though the hut's only window.

Luowski spun in his chair. He looked directly at Maybeck.

38

WHERE IS EVERYBODY? Finn thought. Out of breath, still terrified, he headed toward Monstro as the fireworks began.

While others looked up, Finn happened to be looking out at the water. A Zodiac inflatable boat was chugging well offshore. Finn knew that route. The Zodiac raft was headed for the cabanas.

He had no choice but to go back. His legs shook as he thought about the cobra. About the crewman retching and bending over after Tia Dalma cursed him. About Jafar's anger.

Finn had agreed to take the assignment. Afraid of all that faced him, he headed back beneath a canopy of exploding fireworks.

39

WILLA CREPT UP to the old plane. "Psst!" she hissed.

"In here," came Philby's voice.

She pulled herself up onto the wing and looked down into the cockpit. Philby sat in the torn leather pilot's seat.

"There's no room," she complained.

"My lap," he said, patting his legs.

"As if!"

A brilliant flash lit the sky. Willa jumped into the cockpit. She squeezed in next to Philby, nearly in his lap.

They watched the sky, but not the fireworks. Their attention was focused on the end of the runway and the blackness beyond.

40

LUOWSKI DELIVERED a right fist into Maybeck's abs. The blow hurt. Maybeck faked a left by raising his elbow. It caught Luowski attention. He threw a right into Luowski's ear. The giant kid staggered back, off-balance.

Luowski banged into the radio table. He reached for a black button on the end of a pair of wires crudely attached to a box on the wall. Maybeck didn't know what the boy was doing but he knew he had to stop him.

The off-balance Luowski backhanded Maybeck across the face. He threw a punch, but Maybeck caught the boy's sleeve and tugged. Luowski proved himself even stronger than he looked. Maybeck realized this a second too late. Luowski shoved. Maybeck flew onto the dirt floor.

Luowski banged the button on the wall. The clicking sound it made was familiar to Maybeck, but he couldn't place it.

Luowski tore the wires from the box. Whatever he'd just done, there was no undoing it.

Maybeck scrambled to his feet.

"How'd that work out for you?" Luowski said, cocky and sure of himself.

"About as well as this is going to work out for you," Maybeck fired back. He hurried out of the shed. He shut the door and locked the padlock.

As the padlock clicked, Maybeck recalled where he'd heard the sound that button had made. Bess's barbecue grill.

The igniter.

41

SUDDENLY LINES OF yellow-blue flame ran along either side of the landing strip.

"Gas," Philby muttered.

"You're going to fart?" Willa said, scrambling to get out of the cockpit. Philby held her shirt and pulled her back.

"No, not that! The hose that you and Charlene saw? Same black hose Maybeck and the Cast Member were checking out. They've strung it out along the runway, connected it to propane gas, and set it on fire."

"But why?"

"Landing lights," Philby said, pointing into the dark. "They are using the fireworks as a distraction."

"I don't see a thing," she said.

"No, but we will."

Another few fireworks. A blue wash covered the ocean. From within it appeared an indistinguishable black shape just over the water.

"That's it," Philby said, his voice covered by the low growl of the approaching plane's engines.

42

FINN WATCHED CAST MEMBERS being led from the Zodiac into Tia Dalma's cabana. He heard chanting as he snuck closer to the window.

Six Cast Members. Three girls, three boys. He tried to memorize their faces. Tia Dalma waved a fabric doll in one hand. She hoisted a small carved idol in her other hand. Uttering indistinguishable words in a steady, hypnotizing tone, she stepped closer to the Cast Members.

Finn dropped back down to the sand. He didn't want to fall under whatever spell she was conjuring.

Just the idea of the Overtakers controlling some of the Cast Members turned his stomach. Who could he and the other Keepers trust if not the Cast Members?

On such a warm night, it felt wrong to feel cold on the back of his neck. He spun around quickly.

Maleficent stood at the edge of the jungle. She was looking at Finn.

The six Cast Members left the cabana. A moment later, Finn heard a truck start up. It drove off.

Neither he nor Maleficent had moved. They had not spoken. They stood there, locked in an unending stare.

Finn had always known this moment was coming. But he still felt unprepared.

43

PHILBY AND WILLA scrambled out of the cockpit. They hid in the jungle at the edge of the runway.

"No landing lights," Philby said. "The pilot may have cut the engines. Can barely hear them."

Willa saw only a vague shape. But there was no mistaking the *whop-whop-whop* of the propellers.

Philby pointed to a small but heavy-duty flatbed truck just arriving. Six Cast Members piled out of the truck—three boys and three girls. A girl lit a pair of signal flares. She held them high above her head. Smoke spiraled from the bright orange flares. She waved them in unison.

"They're Cast Members," Willa said. "This can't be something the Overtakers are doing, Philby. Maybe it's something the ship arranged."

"The secrecy doesn't make sense. The propane hoses don't make sense. No landing lights doesn't make sense."

"But they're obviously Cast Members!"

"Who did you see dragging the hoses?" Philby countered.

"Fair," Willa said. "Still doesn't mean you're right."

Philby did not welcome the idea of his being wrong. It wasn't possible. Like math, facts added up to a single result. He could collect any number of facts about a particular thing or event. When added up, the facts told a single truth. Philby spent endless hours collecting such data. When he reached a conclusion, it was as real as simple addition.

"We treat it as hostile," he said. "Cast Members or not."

"Hostile? Seriously?" For a Kingdom Keeper that word held significance. It meant they could be hurt or harmed. It meant they might be killed.

"Whatever is on this plane is being put on that truck and brought to the *Dream*. Right now, you and I are the only ones who know about it."

"So at least one of us has to live to tell the others," she said, her voice quavering.

"That's about right."

44

"CHANGE IS INEVITABLE," Maleficent said. "It is as constant as the setting sun. Change of heart. Change of leadership. Unstoppable as time. Do not blame yourself, Finnegan Whitman. It is not your fault. It is simply the way. This is my moment, not yours. The truth is not always so apparent. For instance, the truth about Wayne Kresky."

What's the truth about Wayne? Finn wondered. He slowly moved away from the cabana. If he could reach the water, swim underwater, maybe her fireballs wouldn't kill him.

"Don't forget, Mr. Disney created me as well," Maleficent said. "He put the same amount of thought into my creation. I am no different. I am entitled to my existence. My beliefs. Order. Obedience. Observation. Whether you admit it or not, you know change is needed. The time has come. Even you can recognize the result of the so-called freedoms allowed in the parks. The sniveling, runny-nosed rats disobeying their parents. The complaining. The impatience. You know exactly what I'm talking about."

He didn't understand why the human body had eyelids that could block out all sight but no way to plug one's ears. He was forced to listen.

"I like the parks the way they are," Finn said. "The way Mr. Disney imagined them."

"Of course you do! But it is not to be. You see?"

"Nope. Don't see that at all. I just saw a plane land. We know about the truck. I saw the six Cast Members. I memorized their faces." It wasn't the perfect truth, but it did the trick.

That seemed to hit her like a landed punch. She held out her hand. A fireball grew in her palm. It stayed there burning. "Do not test me, boy."

"You're a bitter, old hag," Finn said. "You hang around with losers like Cruella De Vil." He couldn't just run for it. He needed the stolen journal. As much as he feared the dark fairy, he'd watched her tuck it into her robe in the library. Maybe she still hid it there. He might not get another chance like this.

"You will not interfere," she said.

"You don't know us so good," Finn said.

"When was the last time you spoke to your mother?" Maleficent's voice crackled with contentment.

Finn couldn't catch his breath.

"It was at the picnic tables, I believe," said the green woman.

They've been watching us!

"I know for certain you have not seen her in the last hour or so."

Finn's eyes teared up. His throat stuck shut.

"Little boy wants his mommy?" Maleficent gloated. "You are older than when we first met. But still foolish. Yes? Naive. I have taken certain precautions to ensure your cooperation."

"Never," he whispered.

"You will, of course, do exactly as I say."

"Will not."

"She is with us. You see? Nothing you can do about it. Just look into her eyes when you next see her. That should be enough."

Green eyes! Finn thought, his mind a whirlpool. His heart a stone. He had done this to her. It was because of him she had come on the cruise. Because of him the twisted, evil creature in front of him had resorted to blackmail. Worse, there appeared to be no way out. He could not conjure, cast spells, or throw fireballs. He was a kid whose image had been used to make a three-dimensional tour guide! He was nothing next to her. *What now?* he wondered. Was he supposed to sabotage his own team to save his mother? Could he bring himself to do that?

Philby would be thinking of ways to get the

journal back. Charlene would be planning the proper way to battle her. Willa would want to outthink her. Maybeck would step up and challenge her face-to-face. Finn wanted his mother. Maleficent was right about that.

He backed up, leading her toward the water and away from the cabanas. An instinctive retreat. *Coward!* He failed to stop his feet. The water passed his knees. It crept higher toward his waist.

As she waded in, Maleficent said, "Let us strike a deal. Your life for your mother's. From the ocean you came. To the ocean you shall return."

Finn had not seen this coming. He thought the deal she would propose for his mother's freedom to be betrayal, disloyalty to his friends. But his life? Was he to die so his mother could live? Even if that were to happen, would Maleficent keep her word?

"Walt Disney not only created characters," Finn said. "He created *roles*. Characters are stuck with their roles. You are not obeying yours. What happens to those who do not obey?"

"Do not twist my words."

"Can a character be smarter or wiser or more important than the one who created her?" Finn was keeping her thinking. He backed up into the water, now waist-deep. He could not trust this *thing* to spare his mother.

There could be no deal. He either used his wits, or all was lost. In any deal someone wants something or possesses something, and the other party must negotiate from strength. What would give him power over her? Did such a thing even exist?

The dark fairy reared back her arm, prepared to throw the fireball. They both understood it was a poor threat. What good was fire with so much water around? Her cape opened. There in the light of the flame he saw the leather-bound journal tucked into her belt.

The water was over her knees as she threw the fireball.

In that moment, it all made sense. Finn understood he would have but one shot to defeat her.

She threw the fireball. Finn ducked underwater, allowing it to fly past where he had stood. He opened his mouth. The seawater rushed in. One big gulp and he would die. His mother might be freed.

Bubbles flowing from his submerged mouth, Finn shouted, "Starfish wise, starfish cries."

45

MAYBECK RAN TOWARD the glow hovering above the landing strip. *The igniter*, he thought. By pushing that button, Luowski had started a fire. Explosions punctuated the sky. The fireworks show was nearing its finale. He hurdled over a fallen palm tree that blocked the narrow path.

He arrived at the far end of the landing strip just as a plane bounced onto the asphalt. Within moments it was at the center of frantic activity. Maybeck sprinted toward the action as Cast Members crowded around the plane. A truck backed up toward the plane's rear door.

He smelled burning rubber. The hose on either side of the asphalt smoldered. The parallel lines stretched into the distance. *So, that's why Cast Members stole the hose.* That was what Luowski had lit. The realization charged Maybeck.

He had made a mistake by locking Luowski inside the hut. The radio was in there. A radio Luowski had used to speak to the pilot. A radio Luowski could still use to talk to the pilot.

As the pilot signaled a Cast Member, shouting

frantically, Maybeck believed that was what had happened. The Cast Member spun around, eyes searching.

Pointing at Maybeck, he called out, "We've got company!"

What now? Maybeck wondered, scanning the area. Seeing the Cast Members confused him. They were allies of the Kingdom Keepers. There was no way they would side with the Overtakers. He and the Keepers had obviously gotten something wrong.

Two of the Cast Members stopped what they were doing. Abandoning the plane, they ran toward Maybeck. *Outnumbered!*

Behind the two a large crate was unloaded from the plane. A group carried it to the waiting truck. The activity stole enough of Maybeck's attention that he was late getting away from the two coming at him.

Just as they were upon him, a streak of color. His two attackers went down. Hard.

Willa had one by the ankles. Philby had knocked down the other.

"We're outta here!" Philby called. He, Maybeck, and Willa took off for the jungle. The two they had tackled sat up, dazed.

The truck's gears complained. The vehicle rumbled and moved off slowly, its contents weighing it down to a crawl.

46

Finn gasped for air as his head punched through the water's surface. Maleficent threw another fireball. Finn ducked.

White foam encircled her. It looked like boiling water. Maleficent, her focus on Finn, took no notice of the water's condition.

Finn spotted a small, pale claw within the foam. Then another. Crabs. Not just hundreds of them, but thousands. Tens of thousands. They surrounded Maleficent.

By the time the dark fairy looked down, an uncommon expression had overcome her: terror. She was standing too deep to move quickly. In a matter of seconds, she began to sink. A hole was being dug into the sand beneath her by ten thousand crabs. The seawater roiled around her like a drain. She extended her arms to swim but screamed as the crabs bit her.

She continued to sink.

Her eyes found Finn and filled with hatred.

"Release my mother, and I'll call them off," he hollered above the sound of the churning water.

Maleficent was now waist-deep.

She spoke a spell, but nothing happened. She pulled the journal from her waist and held it high to keep it dry. She tried the spell again.

Would Triton's crabs drown the fairy? Kill her? In all his dreams of defeating Maleficent, Finn had never wished her dead. The idea sickened him.

He said, "Just release my mother!" He had the power to stop this. He could try the code again.

"She's a mere human!"

What was that supposed to mean?

"You think she did this?" she cried. "Don't be a fool. Is it Ariel? That little bi—"

Finn shouted. "I did this!"

He had never seen such an expression on Maleficent's face. Surprise. Alarm. Fear? Was the dark fairy afraid of the "foolish boy"?

"Give me the journal. Release my mother. I can stop this!"

"You underestimate me," Maleficent called out above the roar. She was chest-deep and sinking. Her lips moved silently. Another spell?

She vanished. One moment up to her chin. The next, the journal fell into the water as a black cormorant appeared on the surface. The bird shook water from its feathers, cawed loudly at Finn, and flew off.

Finn struggled through the surf and snatched up the journal. He shook water from its cover. Around him, the foam receded. Ten thousand crabs dispersed.

Behind him, in the open water, the Zodiac slapped through the waves. Easily identifiable in the bow sat a woman with dreadlocks and square shoulders.

Tia Dalma.

47

A DRIPPING-WET FINN climbed the cabana's stairs. He eased the door open. Empty! No great surprise since he'd seen Tia Dalma in the Zodiac. A massage table had been pushed against the wall. Candles flickered.

He needed to read as much of the journal as possible before taking it onto the ship. Maleficent had stolen it once. It might be stolen again. In his heart and mind there was but a single thought. His mother was under the power of the Overtakers.

Looking down, he saw a pentagram drawn in chalk on the floor. A dead frog was pinned by its limbs in the center of the pentagon. Each triangle contained a small terra-cotta cup. There were dead moths in one. Fish guts in another. A flower floating on oil in a third. Alongside the star was a sock puppet. It was black, with what looked like bat wings. Elbow macaroni formed horns on its head. Hard red wax had formed a puddle on the floorboards.

He moved close to a candle and opened the journal. He believed his mother's survival depended upon whatever was in these pages. To bargain with Maleficent, he had to know why the journal was so important. Wayne had given him hints: a conjuring. A ritual. Chernabog. He shuddered at the thought.

Just as important, he had to understand the journal's contents before Philby or Willa got to it. For the first time ever, he understood the rules had changed. To protect his mother he might have to go it alone.

Some of the writing had smeared because of the seawater. The parts written in pencil were blurred and often illegible. The notes written in ink were clearer. He read about someone named Stravinsky. Finn knew the name—a Soviet general? an athlete? an author? He couldn't place it.

There were pages of sketches that included shooting stars and brooms. He saw sketches of monsters. Mickey's sorcerer's hat. Arrows connected notes to sketches and notes to notes. It read like he was inside someone's head. Many of the notes were numbered and circled. Some carried asterisks. It was beyond Finn. Maybe Philby could piece it together—if Finn dared to share it.

The top corners of the yellowed pages revealed a particularly worn section of the book. He turned pages to reach the section. There was a drawing of Chernabog!

There were some odd notes:

cruel
dominant, frightening, territorial

There were references to instruments:

cymbals/percussion dissonant horns

He studied a drawing of some stone steps. Next a blank page with a carefully drawn hieroglyph in each corner.

On the last of the thumb-worn pages he read from a passage:

Life is because of the gods. With their sacrifice they gave us life. They produce our sustenance which nourishes life.

Finn flipped through more of the well-worn pages.

More notes and arrows and numbers. More musical references. A confusing jumble of gobbledygook.

He started over, carefully reading from the start of the worn pages. He worked hard to memorize their contents. He went through it a third time and fourth. He believed he had most of it committed to memory. If the journal was taken from him, the middle section wouldn't be fully lost.

Translating the meaning of its pages would have to wait for Philby and Willa. Maybe Wayne would be the only one who could understand it all.

As Finn stared at the pages, his mother's face appeared. His mother, the green-eyed Overtaker. His mother, another of Maleficent's captives. Finn recoiled. The journal was filled with strange magic.

The distant sounding of the ship's horn snapped him out of it. The *Dream* was calling.

48

CHARLENE CLUNG TO the spare tire on the truck's undercarriage. She didn't fully remember running to catch up with the departing truck, but there she was.

With each bump she nearly lost her grip. The sounding of the ship's horn signaled the all-aboard. Passengers would be headed back to the ship.

The truck bumped off the asphalt. Charlene fell onto the sand road. The truck pulled away without her. She rolled into the nearby bushes to hide. The rear lights flashed red. The brakes squealed. The truck slowed to a stop then backed up.

Something—someone—was out on the sand road. Charlene tucked deeper into the bushes. It was Willa, out of breath from running behind the truck. Next came Philby, panting and wheezing.

"Psst!" Charlene won their attention. The two hunkered down next to her.

"That was stupid." Willa could barely get a word out.

"It just happened," said Charlene. "Sometimes I can't control myself."

"Why are they doing this?" Philby said. "They're

putting it onto a boat when they could just drive onto the pier and deliver it to the ship."

"That depends on what's in the crate," Charlene said. "Looks like they may be trying to sneak it on."

"If I had to guess," Philby said, "I'd say it's a bear." The girls looked at him skeptically. "Did you see the air holes? Top and bottom. Whatever's in there, it's alive."

49

"**D**O YOU MIND?" Finn asked the man in uniform who occupied the concierge desk in the deck's private lounge. Finn pointed to the copier.

"Not at all. It's there for our Concierge guests."

The lounge had two TVs, eight or ten café tables, a fully stocked buffet, espresso machine, and small refrigerator. With the lounge's ten o'clock closing time quickly approaching, the concierge and Finn found themselves alone.

Finn put the first of the journal's worn pages onto the printer/copier's glass reader. He pulled the lid down as far as it would go. He touched the copy button. The machine issued grinding sounds.

It spit out a blank page. He tried again with the same result.

"Could you help me, please? I'm doing something wrong." He didn't want the concierge to see the old journal, but making a copy was too important.

The man had no reaction to the leather-bound journal. He did exactly as Finn had done. A third blank page slipped from the machine.

"Strange." He checked the settings and tried again. No different. He tried copying another page from the journal. Same thing. "Must be broken," he said. Then he replaced the journal with the ship's daily calendar of events.

It copied

"Even stranger," the concierge said. "It seems to be something to do with the book itself. Maybe a special ink?"

Maybe magic, Finn was thinking. He thanked the man and headed to Maybeck's room. Philby joined them a few minutes later. Maybeck's aunt Bess, a strong supporter of the Kingdom Keepers, made an excuse and left the boys alone.

Finn explained everything from the crabs nearly drowning Maleficent to her flying off as a cormorant. His recovering the journal and the strange pentagram drawn on the floor of the cabana. He left out the part about his mother now being an Overtaker. He spoke strongly of the need to replicate the pages and how the copier had failed.

"I was thinking you could copy them by hand," he told Maybeck. "Your being the artist and all."

"No problem," Maybeck said. He took out some art supplies and got to work.

As he started to write the first line the tip of his

pencil broke. "Dang! I barely touched it to the page." He tried again with another pencil. It snapped in half. Frustrated, he picked up a pen. All its ink leaked out onto the page the moment the nib touched the paper. Maybeck grabbed his phone. It didn't have cell service, but the camera would work.

The photo was of a blank page.

"Not possible," he muttered.

"Interesting," Philby said.

"Magic," said Finn. "It's dark magic."

The two looked at him strangely.

"Cursed. A spell. Something. Whatever is on these pages is only for the person who possesses the journal."

"That's possible," Philby whispered. "But that has to be some serious magic."

Finn reminded them both about what Wayne had told him about the journal's contents. How they had something to do with Chernabog.

Philby gasped. Color drained from his face.

"What's going on?" Finn asked.

Philby whispered harshly. "It's not a bear."

50

Finn was walking the passageway of Deck 8. Stateroom doors flanked the starboard wall. A long corridor that looked more like an endless tunnel. A familiar voice called from behind. "Why are you avoiding me?" Not just any voice. His mother's.

He couldn't turn around. He couldn't face her. But he did. She held a power over him more like gravity than motherhood. From this distance, she looked the same. The mom he'd known before Maleficent had told him about her conversion.

"You haven't been back to our suite since the barbecue." She sounded crushed. *Tricks*, Finn thought.

"Maybeck asked me over for the night. We going to watch a movie. Bess is fine with it," he lied. That didn't feel right.

"Why?"

"You're not yourself." It spilled out. Finn hadn't meant to say it.

"You will not address me like that, young man."

She stepped forward. He took a step back. The overhead light hit her eyes. They were green. Finn caught the vomit in his mouth and swallowed the bitter taste.

Another step toward him. Finn stood his ground. The thing was, Finn wanted to hug her. He wanted to help her. This woman who had helped him through so much. He didn't move, allowing her to slowly close the distance between them.

"All she wants is the journal," she said.

Finn's stomach warned him of another visit from his dinner.

"Help me, Finn."

"I want to."

"Is it so difficult?"

"I don't have the journal." Another lie. "She kind of melted in the waves. You can ask her. She dropped it. There were all these crabs. Maybe they ate it. Maybe it sank. I don't know."

"I thought we were a team," she said, sensing the lie.

The strings inside his chest tightened. He winced. "We are," he said.

"A pretty good one."

He nodded.

"Then why would you lie to me?" she said.

Her words slapped him in the face. Head versus heart. A history shared. He didn't answer. He couldn't. She took a step closer.

Tears ran down his cheeks. "Gotta go," he said. "I've always been on your side. Always will be."

A couple squeezed past them. Finn felt invisible. It was only him and this woman who'd once been his mother.

"I'm going to make it right," he said.

There were tears in his mother's eyes, too. He couldn't stand it when she cried.

She knows that! he reminded himself. *Tricks!*

She was close enough to grab hold of him. Too close.

"Tell her I don't have it," he repeated. Until he could figure out how to trade for his mother, he had to keep up the lie.

"She won't believe it. Neither do I."

Finn ran away. It was unfair to his mom. But what choice did he have? She was the enemy—his mother was the enemy—and he had no idea what to do about it.

51

WHY DO I FEEL SO ALONE? Charlene thought. She had gone on solo assignments before. Why did this one feel so different?

It was just past midnight as her hologram stood in front of the "Cast Members Only" door. The door led to the backstage area of the Walt Disney Theatre. Philby had managed to cross her over using the DHI backup computer installed by Storey Ming. She had gone to sleep wearing the white Cast Member shorts, a powder-blue polo, and white sneakers. Her blond hair was pulled back in a black scrunchy to keep it out of her eyes if things got interesting.

Once she was inside, the corridor was narrow. Her projection held strong, which only made sense since she and the DHI hosts had already been on the theater's stage.

The carpet, indoor-outdoor stuff, felt spongy under-foot. Charlene practiced controlling her DHI. She reached out and took hold of the shiny gray banister. She let go, focused, and waved her hologram through the same metal handrail. It provided her with a sense of much-needed security and confidence. If she kept her head when attacked she could remain a 3-D projection of light. Her adversaries could not harm her.

Her assignment was to locate the crate and determine its contents. Sally Ringwald had told Finn that the crate had been off-loaded from a small boat and taken into the theater. It was as much as she knew. The rest was up to Charlene.

She spotted a security camera extending from the wall. She nodded, knowing Philby was watching her. She passed several dressing rooms, a bathroom, and some makeup rooms. Her surroundings grew darker as she moved beyond a stairway leading down. Darker still as she stepped into the wings. Here, props were tied to the floor with wide straps. Backstage lanes were marked by bright yellow-and-black warning tape.

The overhead stage lights flashed red. She wasn't sure what it meant but took it as a signal. Either for her, or for others. Was it a warning from Philby? A technician working the lights? She curled herself into one of the side curtains. It was like wrapping herself in a beach towel. She left a small crack to peer through.

Two girls dressed all in black hurried past. *Stage crew*, she thought. A moment later two ragged-looking dogs followed on the heels of the girls.

Not dogs, Charlene realized. *Hyenas.*

The flash of red lights had been a warning for every-one backstage!

She hurried in the opposite direction. Reaching the stairs, she paused as she heard voices. Anger bubbled up from down there.

The metal stairs angled as steep as a ladder. She arrived at the bottom landing. The voices were much stronger and clearer. *Close!*

As a Keeper, Charlene had practiced dealing with anxiety. Long, slow, deep breaths. Inhale through the nose. Exhale out the mouth. Think calm thoughts: a sunset, a song.

She peered into a crowded space. The walls and the ceiling crawled with pipes and wire caddies. There were Day-Glo orange caution triangles and more of the yellow-and-black caution tape. Rubber tubes connected to metal cylinders. A gated wire mesh platform faced her. It looked like an elevator of some kind. Looking up at the ceiling, she understood more about the platform. It was one of three lifts that serviced trapdoors in the overhead stage. Props and actors could appear and disappear onstage.

The mesh lift held the wooden crate. It stood tall like an obelisk. Several workmen were gathered around the lift. They appeared neither concerned nor excited. Bored, was more like it.

Charlene summoned her courage. She took a deep breath. She entered the room.

"Everything going okay in here?" she asked, directing her words to one of the men wearing blue coveralls. *I'm a Cast Member. I'm important. They need to answer me.*

The man leaned back on the upside-down plastic bucket he was sitting on. He waved his hand. "No problem here." He was Indonesian or Indian with a thick, singsong voice. "Turns out the straps are not of the proper length. We could double them up, but the commodore said it is not regulation. So, we are waiting. Always waiting. What was that up there? The red light. The running."

"It was nothing," she said. *The commodore,* she thought. Who was that? "Can I get the straps for you?"

"It has been taken care of," the crewman said.

She bravely entered and circled the crate. Philby would want to know everything. Its corners were screwed shut, not nailed. The plywood was thick, though new. It still held the sweet pine smell of freshly sawed lumber. But a sour smell competed with it. There were holes the size of sand dollars cut into its top and bottom. The holes were covered with a fine black mesh.

From within came the sound of something breathing. Something big. Something that was giving off that smell. For a moment she lost her DHI to fear. Deep breath.

There was a grouping of four bolts on opposite sides of the crate.

Heavy black arrows were stenciled onto the crate. THIS SIDE UP, they read.

Suddenly a deep red light flashed from the wall.

Two of the four men jumped to their feet. "What the hello?" the lead worker said. "That can't happen. There is no show under way!"

"Everything okay?" Charlene asked.

The light stopped flashing, and the workers noticeably relaxed.

The other man standing said, "Someone musta hit it by mistake."

The man with the sweet voice told Charlene, "It is the lift signal. It comes from the stage level warning us to stand clear. But with no show going on, it makes little sense it should flash."

"Should I take a look?" Charlene asked. *Philby*, she thought. Another warning.

There was no need to push things further. If it was a warning from Philby, it was best to get out while she could.

"I'll be back in a half hour," she said, thinking it made her sound more important.

"As you like," said the leader.

Out in the narrow hall, she froze as she heard

footfalls coming quickly down the stairs. The speed, the intensity signaled some sort of trouble. She could feel it in her bones. She looked up the stairs.

"Julia!" It was a girl's voice, directed at Charlene. "You're wanted upstairs immediately!" A second girl's voice. This one familiar.

Two girls in silhouette, halfway up. She had called Charlene *Julia*. When they saw her face they would realize she wasn't the person they expected. She was in trouble.

The two girls turned. Their faces caught some light.

Charlene's throat tightened. She could hardly breathe.

Amanda and Jess looked down at her. Their bodies showed a faint blue outline in places. Barely visible, Charlene knew what caused such artefacts.

They were holograms.

52

"**W**HY SHOULD I HAVE IT?" Philby asked Finn. With his mother off playing bingo, he and Finn were alone in the suite.

"You need to keep it," Finn said.

"Because?"

"No questions, please. Just do it for me." Finn passed the leather-bound journal to Philby.

"I don't get it," Philby said.

"You don't have to get it. You just have to take care of it. Put it in the room's safe. Hide it. Whatever you want. I don't care. Just keep it away from me."

"Why are you acting so strange?"

"Listen, I told Maleficent that it sank. That it's gone. Lost. But I don't think she believed me."

"This was when?" Philby sounded choked. "You and Maleficent? Since when?"

He'd told his mother, not Maleficent, though the lie was out there. "Thing is, they're going to come after me, Philby. For the journal, I mean. As far as they're concerned, if anyone has it, it's me. See? So, I can't have it. And I can't know where it is. I can't know anything about it. One spell and I could tell them everything."

Philby's Wave Phone buzzed, winning his attention. It spared Finn from having to provide any more of an answer. *Because I'm going to trade it for my mother. And then everything we've done is for nothing.* "It's from Charlie. You're not going to believe this." Finn didn't care about the box brought aboard. He didn't care about what the pentagram in Tia Dalma's bungalow meant. Not unless it had to do with his mother. Philby furiously typed a return text into the phone. He looked up at Finn. "Open the door. You're not going to believe it."

"Seriously?" A reluctant and impatient Finn did as he was asked. Coming toward him from down the hall were three girls. He had expected to see Charlene. But Amanda and Jess? "How did you . . . ? How can this . . . ?" Amanda stepped close like she might want to *kiss* him. *In front of everyone!* She walked right through him.

A stunned Finn addressed Philby. "You did this and didn't tell us?"

"Wasn't me!"

Everyone piled into the room. The door swung shut.

"Of course it was you," Finn said angrily. "Why lie about it?"

"It was . . . is . . . Wayne," Amanda explained. "Jess and I are asleep at Mrs. Nash's. Wayne crossed us over here—"

Finn remembered Amanda asking him how he would feel if she and Jess came on the cruise. He had dismissed it as silly. She, Jess, and Wayne had been planning this for a long time.

"Using the backup server in the Radio Studio," Philby said, interrupting.

"Exactly," Amanda said. "That's why he put the extra computer onto the ship."

"Not as backup for our holograms," Finn said. "But to send backup *for* us." He tried to process it all. "Blue artefacts," he said, noticing the shimmer at the edges of their projections.

"Makes sense," Philby said. "The new update requires massive computing power. The server in the Radio Studio isn't nearly powerful enough. Their projections are an older version of the software."

"Glad to see us?" Amanda said, looking squarely at Finn. He didn't answer, too caught up in trying to figure out what Wayne was up to. Amanda looked crestfallen.

"They got me out of the basement. The theater. Things were getting iffy." Charlene thanked Philby for the warning lights.

"You saw the box?" Philby said.

Charlene lowered her voice. "Eight feet tall. Holes at the bottom and the top. Screens across the holes. And it smelled bad. Like a wet dog."

"More hyenas?" Finn said.

"You wish! If it had been lying on its side, maybe. But it was standing up." She described the four bolts on either side. She looked at Philby, hoping for answers.

"We think it's Chernabog. The holes were at the bottom or the top of the box?" Philby asked.

Charlene explained. "More of them at the top."

"It's a bar," Philby said. "The bolts are holding a bar inside the box. It's definitely Chernabog."

"You know this, how?" Finn said, challenging Philby. He felt exhausted. He was wasting his time. None of this mattered any longer.

"Because bats sleep hanging upside down," Philby said. There was a clock ticking faintly somewhere in the room. A baby was crying down the hall. The sloshing of seawater against the hull came rhythmically and steadily.

"Half bull, half bat," Finn whispered. For a brief few seconds, he wasn't thinking about his mother. Instead, he remembered being in school with Mr. E. as they discussed the mythic creature.

Amanda's eyes burned into him. She looked angry and scared. He felt like he'd done something wrong. He couldn't think what it could have been.

53

THE NEXT TWO DAYS were spent at sea as the *Dream* steamed toward a Caribbean island. Finn avoided his mother, sleeping on a couch in Maybeck's suite. Knowing she liked the more formal dining rooms, he ate in the Deck 11 cafeteria, Cabanas, keeping watch for her. Amanda and Jess crossed over onto the ship at eleven each night. They remained aboard for a few hours as Jess searched the ship for images that might match her recent dreams. Amanda kept watch on Philby's suite, prepared to use her *push* ability to keep the journal safe.

Finn had yet to come up with a decent strategy for how to rescue his mother. The journal was clearly connected to Chernabog. Possibly Tia Dalma was involved. He hadn't seen Luowski or Sally Ringwald since the island. He wondered if they were hiding on the ship or had gone back to the mainland with the plane. If he traded the journal for his mother, it would be akin to treason. If Maleficent intended to supercharge Chernabog using a spell cast by Tia Dalma, then the journal could *never* be allowed into her hands.

Standing at the railing of Deck 13's Goofy's Sports

Deck made him feel like he was flying over the ocean. Wind whipped his face.

"You okay?" It was Storey in her Cast Member outfit. Finn didn't answer.

"You want company, or should I go?" she asked.

"Whatever," Finn said, staring down at the foaming water breaking from the hull.

"I can help," she said.

"I really don't think so," Finn said.

"I was working the Concierge Sun Deck," she said. "One of the waiters spilled ice water down your mom's back. Her sunglasses fell off."

Finn didn't need to ask. *Green eyes*, he thought. So, his secret was out. "I haven't told the others," he said.

"That's up to you." She stood alongside Finn at the railing. Looked out at a horizon without land. "We're a long way from anywhere."

"Maleficent and I had a moment."

"Okay."

"She wants the journal."

"No matter what she tells you, she won't change your mother back," Storey said.

"I know." Finn felt desperate and so alone.

"The Imagineers believe the OTK spell wears off in time. It won't last forever."

Finn stood up straighter and looked at Storey. The

red tips of her hair danced in the endless wind. The ship traveled at over twenty miles per hour. "Since when are you and the Imagineers so close?" Finn said.

"Are you asking for my résumé? Sorry, I don't carry it with me. There's a lot you don't know about me, Finn. Have you ever heard of the Barracks?"

She might as well have punched him. Amanda and Jess had been kept against their wills at the Barracks. They had escaped to Orlando. "You're talking about my friends?" He was worried the two were in danger.

"Who are your friends? No. I'm talking about the Barracks."

"I know about the Barracks. Yes," he said. He'd already given her more information than was necessary.

"Good. Then maybe that tells you something about me. Maybe it doesn't."

Girls from the Barracks—it was mostly girls—had unusual abilities. Amanda could *push*. Jess could dream bits and pieces of the future. Was Storey trying to claim she had unusual abilities?

She was right. He didn't know enough about her. It suddenly felt as if he couldn't trust her, either. She was working too hard to earn that trust.

"Who are your friends?" she asked.

"Never mind."

"I want to help. I'm here to help," she said, nearly

quoting exactly what Jess and Amanda had said when they'd showed up as holograms.

"He's going to a lot of trouble," Finn said.

"Mr. Kresky?" Storey's saying his name flooded Finn with heat. *How can she know Wayne?*

"He has a daughter," Finn said, testing her.

"Wanda," Storey said.

Finn felt dizzy. He pushed away from the railing.

"You okay?"

"You just asked me that. I didn't answer. I'm not okay. No."

"I want to help," she said.

"Uh-huh. I don't have it," he said. "I don't know where it is."

"Don't know where what is?"

"Nice try," Finn said. "The thing is, I can't trust myself. So, how can I trust you? Or anyone, for that matter? When you stop trusting yourself, who's left? There's stuff going down that I can't talk about. You're not going to get me to talk about it."

"Like your mother?"

"Like my mother. Yes. Okay? You know my deep, dark secret. What are you going to do about it?"

"I'm going to help," she said. She sounded so calm, so reassuring.

"It's hopeless, Storey. I can't win. I can't fix things.

Since becoming a DHI, I've always been able to fix things. Not everything, but the stuff that counts. Usually. You know. Here and there. But this? Not this? Not me, not you. Not her."

"Your mother or Maleficent?"

"Both. I'm losing. I'm the one losing. I don't like losing."

"But you haven't lost," she said.

"You think?" he said stridently. "How do you figure?"

"She wants something from you. What does she want?"

Finn looked into her eyes. Dark brown. Deep. Concerned. He still didn't trust her. "No," he said.

"Stand still," she said. "Can you do that for me?"

"What's this about?"

Storey took a step forward. Finn flinched. "Don't move. Don't freak out." She carefully, slowly, placed her open hand upon his cheek and part of his neck. Her hand wasn't on him but a second. It was warm. It felt strangely good. She pulled it away. Lowered her arm. When they next met eyes, hers appeared far more troubled than they had only a moment earlier. "Trust me," she said.

Finn looked past Storey to see a puzzled Charlene watching them. Storey's hand remained gently on Finn's cheek. The two of them eye to eye. It looked all wrong to Charlene. She took off in a hurry.

"She'll tell Amanda," Finn choked out. "We're kind of . . . We're friends."

Storey pushed back from Finn, her face alarmed. Finn didn't understand her reaction, but then again, he couldn't figure out much about girls. "I knew a girl named Amanda," Storey said. "Not exactly a common name."

"Pretty common," Finn said, having no idea where this was going, or whom to trust.

"She was tight with this other girl, Jessica. This was in the Barracks. The place I told you about."

"Is that right?" Finn said, trying hard to disguise what he knew.

"They escaped maybe two years before I did."

"Escaped? That sounds a little dramatic." Finn knew all about their escape. It had been perilous. But he worried that Storey was suddenly looking for information more than making conversation.

"It *was* dramatic. And dangerous," she said. "And if they hadn't done that, I would never have tried it, too." Her eyes glazed. Finn wondered if anyone could be that good an actor. "I owe my freedom to them."

"You were there with them," Finn whispered.

Storey looked incredulous. "Have you heard anything I've said?"

54

THE BOOMING VOICE of the ship's director of entertainment rang out. "Please join me in welcoming the cast of Disney's own Disney Hosts Interactive!" The stage of the Walt Disney Theatre looked out at fifteen hundred people. They jumped to their feet. Excited faces. Waving hands.

"Thank you!" Finn said, through the wireless microphone. He spoke the memorized script. It was short and sweet. An enthusiastic message of harmony and magic. He told them that he and the others would be autographing cruise posters after the program. Charlene announced that their DHI holograms would be on Deck 11 later that evening for tours and photographs. The crowd went wild.

The stage went dark as a short video celebrating the DHIs ran on the auditorium's three screens.

A fishing net fell from the stage rafters. It covered the five Keepers. They struggled to get free. A team of five pirates converged on them. The pirates pushed the trapped kids back a few feet. The stage dropped out from under them all, moving like an elevator.

A spotlight revealed Maleficent standing stage right. Her green face filled the three screens.

The already cheering crowd grew louder. She raised her hand. A fireball appeared. The crowd could not contain itself. Maleficent hurled the fireball. It streaked over the heads of the audience like a comet. It burned out and was gone.

"SILENCE!" she roared. The audience settled. Quickly. "SIT DOWN!" They obeyed.

Maleficent's determined expression never faltered. "Behold the New Order." Her voice was eerily calm. "The dawning of a new age." Whispers within the crowd. "Enough of all this prince-and-princess spun-sugar nonsense. It's time for the Grimm in the fairy tales to express itself. The woods are dark, my dears. The beasts within them will eat you for supper, not sing you a song. Wake up and smell the roasted."

As the elevator descended, the last thing Finn saw was an audience in confusion. They didn't know how to respond. Maleficent sounded so serious. Overhead, the trapdoor shut. Finn and the others were in a small room.

Charlene said, "This is where I was before!"

The Overtakers had just captured the Keepers in broad daylight, in front of a live audience.

There was no tear-jerking speech. No end-of-the-movie apology or dramatic summary. The pirates drove their swords through the net, intending to stab the kids and kill them dead.

The Keepers saw the blades coming. Finn dodged the one intended for him. Maybeck reached through the net and pulled a pirate whose sword was aimed at Willa off balance. Charlene kicked the net and knocked over another pirate.

But it was Philby, clever Philby, who grabbed the arm holding the sword coming at him. He pulled the sword hard and sliced open the net.

Philby held open the slice. Maybeck followed Willa out of the net. Finn was next. He ducked below a sword swipe. The blade lodged in the wood of a towering crate. Eight feet high. It had holes cut top and bottom.

Chernabog!

Willa snagged a shield from the *Lion King* show. She blocked her pirate's sword, then lunged and pushed the man. He stumbled. Maybeck thumped the man with a length of pipe. The guy fell to his knees, then onto his face.

Seven pirates became five. Then three. Charlene threw a few moves on one of those remaining. She did a back handspring into him, sending him to the floor. Finn stood next to the giant box. "Help me!" he called out.

Charlene and Maybeck put their shoulders against

the crate. Philby joined them. It teetered. Rocked. But returned upright.

"Again!" Finn called.

The crate went over. Seeing the crate hit, the scallywags took off running. It should have meant something to the Keepers when the pirates all fled at once.

The wood shattered. The box broke open.

A horrid thing lay there. Its black skin was leathery. It had the fingers of a gorilla. Reddish-brown hair grew from its neck and limbs, though its wings remained smooth and clear. Its awful face was a mixture of bull and bat. A horrible, ugly-looking thing with two scarred black horns. They bent and curved from its skull above large, hairy ears pointed like a bat's.

It was gigantic, the size of a refrigerator. Its arms were as thick as pythons.

Its eyes squinted and opened. Red as blood. As bottomless as the ocean.

Someone screamed.

It was Philby.

55

THE KEEPERS ESCAPED the lower-level theater room as a group. They ran fast. Up the stairs. Through the door to the public area of the ship. Down companionways. Through more doors. Up more stairs. Along decks.

They found their way to their staterooms and locked the doors. They hid under the covers and shivered.

None of them could sleep. Just knowing the beast was on board was enough to make their hearts race and fry their brains. They had released Chernabog from his crate! The Overtakers would now feel the need to speed up whatever plan they had in mind. At the top of that agenda was certain to be the elimination of the Keepers. The pirates' swords had failed. It would now be all-out war. Tonight. Before the Keepers had a chance to regroup.

Finn understood but didn't care. All that mattered was reversing the OTK spell on his mother. By this point, if he'd had the journal, he would have surrendered it to Maleficent. He needed not only a plan, but a backup plan because Maleficent was certain to double-cross him.

A knock on the door to Maybeck's room startled Finn. Maybeck and Bess had managed to doze off. "I'll get it," he said softly.

It was Storey. Finn stepped into the hall. He held the door open slightly.

"You?" Finn said.

"Take me to Jess and Amanda," she said.

"I don't know who you mean."

"Now, or I can't help you," Storey said. "And don't be cute about it. We both know who they are and what they can do."

"What if it's a trap?" Finn said.

"Excuse me?"

"You seem to know a lot and then claim to know nothing."

"Listen to me, Finn. All the security cameras went dead backstage in the Walt Disney Theatre. This happened right after the unscheduled appearance of Maleficent. The unscheduled disappearance of you and your buddies. You're alive. We weren't sure about that. So, that's the good news. The bad news is . . . well . . . either you know it, or you don't know it." She meant the release of Chernabog, but Finn wasn't going to say it, and neither was she. That made him trust her more. "They are either going to go into hiding, or they are going to strike first. Either way, your mother loses out."

"Tell me about it," Finn said.

"I need Jess and Mandy," she said, using Amanda's nickname. Now he trusted her even more. *Maybe she isn't lying.* "If my plan is going to work—"

"What plan?" he asked.

"I told you I would help you. I don't know about you, but I keep my word."

"Snap." Finn had a choice to make. "They are DHIs. Wayne arranged it. They cross over around eleven, so they should be on board by now. Jess wanders, looking for clues. Amanda—Mandy—stands guard. Since our rooms are all on the same passageway, I would think she would be somewhere near the stairs and elevators, but I can't be sure."

"That's all I needed."

"If Charlene told her about us, you and me, then . . . you know. Things might not go so great."

"There is no 'us,'" Storey said. "Eww."

"What's your plan?" Finn asked, feeling hurt and conflicted. "Because I've been making my own."

"I guarantee you mine is better."

"I doubt it."

"I'm five steps ahead of you."

"You aren't," he said.

Storey looked into his eyes. Hers were a rich brown, the color of milk chocolate. There were green specks in her pupils. Finn couldn't look away. She spoke deliberately slowly, her voice somewhere between a whisper and a breath. 'Life is because of the gods. With their sacrifice they gave us life. They produce our sustenance, which nourishes life.'"

Finn's chest tightened. "How can you—? How's that possible?"

"I'm telling you. You have to trust me." Storey pushed Finn back through the door and shut it on him.

Finn found himself in the dark bedroom. A few tiny electronic lights glowed from cabinets and the wall. He heard Bess snoring and Maybeck breathing deeply. "I'm awake," Maybeck said. "Can't sleep. Who was that?"

"I'm awake, but I think I'm dreaming," said Finn. "More a nightmare than a dream."

"You're scared," Maybeck said.

"I am," Finn said, afraid to admit it. But not for the reasons Maybeck thought. Not for anything or anyone other than his mother.

"Same," Maybeck said. "That thing, that animal . . . Who's supposed to stop it?"

Finn had the answer, but he couldn't speak it aloud. *We are.*

56

"Why the engine room?" Willa asked Finn once they were inside a Cast Member freight elevator. Finn pressed the LL button for Lower Level. He had barely slept. Breakfast had been an orange juice. His clothes were starting to smell. He refused to go to his own room. He didn't want to confront his mother.

"The engine deck is the warmest place on the ship," he said. "I'm trying to think like Tia Dalma."

"Interesting," she said. "I'd feel safer if I was a hologram."

"Same."

The elevator landed. They descended a set of ladder-stairs. Finn heaved open a heavy door. A waft of stuffy hot air engulfed them.

The engine deck was spit-shine clean. The machinery was painted and polished. The area stretched the length of the ship. Fire and water bulkheads separated sections at regular intervals. There were valves, switches, and signs throughout. The lighting was bright. The sound, intense. The heat, permeating.

"It's an electric ship," Willa said. "Do you know that?"

Finn had never given it any thought. Nor did he care. But Willa, usually so quiet, talked incessantly when nervous.

"There are three major generators. Each one can make enough electricity to power a small city. Electric motors spin the propellers. They also power the lights, air-conditioning, theaters, galleys, computers, TVs. It's basically a floating power plant. Three, in case one fails. Two backups and one at work."

Finn felt a chill.

The Overtakers understood that holograms were projections of light. They required electricity.

"If Tia Dalma is down here," Willa said, "it won't be easy finding her."

"Philby couldn't see her on any of the security videos. That means she came onto the ship and disappeared. Should we split up?"

"I'd rather not," Willa said. "But I suppose it makes sense given how huge it is. Someone's going to come down here at some point. It's not like we have a lot of time."

"You go that way," he said, pointing forward. "I'll take the aft."

She nodded. "How do we signal each other?"

"Scream, I guess." He had meant it as a joke, but Willa nodded.

"I'm good at that," she said.

Finn moved toward the loudest sound. Somewhere, far to the stern, the propellers spun. He searched behind large tanks and heavy machinery. He stopped and listened. He knelt and looked.

Ten minutes later, he stepped through the final bulkhead and into an area where an eighteen-inch-diameter steel driveshaft spun. It looked to be fifty feet long. It was mounted into a monstrous motor the size of a small house.

Finn saw her legs, first. A waft of smoke, second. She was ignoring the NO SMOKING AT ANY TIME sign.

Tia Dalma sat on a makeshift throne. The closer he came to her the more the hot air smelled of incense and birds. Things earthy and dark and different.

Her rich brown skin shimmered with sweat. She had two gold teeth, a nose ring, myriad loops in her ears. She held a black wooden staff. The carvings reminding him of Jafar.

She clapped lifelessly. "Well done, mon!" She exhaled slowly. The smoke curled. "I be quite the surprised. Your ingenuity, it is. Impressive."

He heard her chanting something at once rhythmic and hypnotic. He refused to listen.

If she'd been trying to put a spell on him, it didn't stick.

216

"I saw the pentagram," he said. "On the floor of the cabana."

She squinted at him. "Did you now? What does ye think? Am I not quite the artist?"

"I think you were trying to make sure Chernabog got off the plane safely."

"Oh, now you're just braggin'. Should you be fixin' to make trouble," she said, "I might advise you reconsider."

"I'm *fixin'* to stay alive," said Finn.

She laughed. "Important to some, yes. Though there are definitely benefits to immortality, I must say. There be a time and place fer everyt'ing, mon," she growled. Such a low voice for a woman. "Would you not agree?"

"We all have our roles to play," he said. "The journal. The book from the library. I have it."

"You know dem Louisiana cicadas—da bug, da insect—only present themselves once every thirteen years? Or is it fifteen? Never the matter. Spirits are like that. Can be. Have their own sense of time."

"You're talking about waking up Chernabog."

"Ah, he's awake all right. Believe thee that! Thanks to you and yours disturbing him and such."

"We didn't know."

"You should have. Like waking a sleeping lion, that one is."

"I'll trade the journal for my mother. Maleficent will know what that means."

"Ye think I'm stupid? Ignorant? You are out of your skivvies, mon. You be playing a game that ain't no game. Not when you're mortal and we ain't."

"You are stuck in a role. I'm not," he said. He'd given the same argument to Maleficent. It had frightened her. Worth a try on this character.

"Looking to broaden my role." Gold teeth crowded Tia Dalma's smile. "Break the chain of indifference and improve my performance."

"It doesn't work like that."

"And ye would be the one to tell me how dem things work?" She chuckled. "Is that so?"

Finn hoped she couldn't see his legs shaking. "A meeting. Her and me. The journal after she frees my mother."

Willa stepped through the bulkhead and into the area. The only way Finn knew was the shift in Tia Dalma's dark eyes.

"Welcome, lass," she said.

"You found her," Willa said.

"She won't give me an answer," Finn said.

"So clever, the two of you, eh?" Tia Dalma said in her slow, bored tone. "I ought to turn you into cockroaches and watch you slither into the shadows."

Finn swallowed dryly. *She can probably do that.*

"You need the journal," Finn said. "You are the one who does the conjuring, am I right? Maleficent can't do it. She needs you. You need the journal. That means you need me."

"You do not possess that of which you speak. You be too smart for that, boy. I could twist you, tie you in a knot, if I want. I can make you tell me anything I wish to hear. Including lies. Including where the book is. Might save us a good deal of time were I to do so. Or I could play with your friend here." She looked intently at Willa. "Plenty of fun to be had in that enterprise, eh? My little doll."

"But you haven't," Finn said. "You've done none of that. Why is that?" She said nothing. "I'll tell you why. You don't know if this is me you are looking at, or a hologram. A real person, or a ghost."

"And you're afraid of ghosts," Willa said, stepping forward.

For an instant, Tia Dalma looked not herself. She flinched. Finn thought Willa had hit a spot. A voodoo queen would have seen her fair share of ghosts. Maybe one or more of those encounters had made her afraid of them.

"I will need a signal," Finn told her. "A way for me to know the meeting has been set up. It will need to be out in the open. Starboard side of the walking deck. Eight o'clock, when everyone is at the show or watching a movie. I will wait five minutes. Maleficent brings my mother. After five minutes I will leave. You won't get the journal."

"When you see dem birds cross the sun when it sets. That will be the night. Do not bother, you no see dem birds."

You can do that? Finn was eager to ask. But of course she could. The heat was making him sweat. Or maybe it was the woman. Maybe that he didn't have much of a plan worked out. Impatience had gotten the better of him.

"You come as a ghost," Tia Dalma said, "it is no deal."

"I will come however I want to come," Finn said. He didn't recognize his own voice. His mother's predicament had changed him. Strength, unbending and willful. He wondered if this was how Maybeck felt all the time.

57

TWO EVENINGS LATER, Finn was on the deck outside the Vibe at sunset when a massive flock of birds crossed in front of the setting sun. Instead of being a thing of beauty, it terrified him.

He turned to see Storey standing there. Wind whipped their hair. "Here you go." She handed him the journal.

"But how?" he said, incredulous. "You told Philby?"

"I did not," she explained. "He knows nothing of it. I promised you, Finn. I take a promise seriously."

"But that's impossible. Philby is the only one who knew where it was. I didn't even know."

"I think that's true," she said.

"Then you're lying. You had to have talked to him to get it."

"I'm not lying. I didn't speak with Philby. I didn't tell him your plans."

"You mean my betraying him. Betraying all the Keepers."

"It's your decision. Don't question it, Finn. Accept it."

"How did you find this?" he asked, squeezing the journal. "How can I trust you if you won't tell me?"

"This doesn't answer you, but I connected with Jess and Amanda. Amanda is mad at you apparently. Mad at *us.*" *There is no "us,"* Finn wanted to remind her. "Jess sketched some of this."

"Some of what?"

"Deck Four. The walking track. Maleficent."

"So, I meet her?" His voice quavered. "Tonight."

"That's what I'm trying to tell you. Yes, you meet her."

"And you're not going to tell me who wins," he said.

"You know how Jess's dreams go. They are rarely complete."

"I do this. I give her the journal. I betray my friends. Everything I've worked for."

"Things done out of love are different. Forgivable. Besides, maybe you win?"

"Against her," he said, doubting himself. "She will double-cross me."

"So, be ready for that."

"With all my superpowers," he said sarcastically. "The only chance I've got is to be a hologram, a DHI, and Tia Dalma said that's a deal breaker."

"And I repeat: Be ready for that."

"Is that all you can say?"

"No," she said. "But it may be all that you need to hear."

"I don't get you," he said. "You've got to be lying."

"You're not listening," she said. "Look what you're holding. What's in your hands? That's the truth. I brought you that truth. Truth wins, Finn."

"Maleficent doesn't know anything about the truth."

"So, teach her," Storey said.

"You don't get it. She tried to kill me. She wants us all dead and out of the way. I just want her to go back to her cosplay."

Storey laughed. "Good one."

"There's nothing to stop her from double-crossing me," he said.

"There's you."

"Even if I get her to release my mom from the Green Eyes first. Once I hand over the journal, she can turn her right back again. Or cast a spell onto me and turn me into flea on the back of a seagull."

"If you don't have a plan, I suppose that's true."

"Will you be there?" he asked.

"I'll be wherever you tell me to be," she said. "Wherever you need me to be."

"Touching my face," Finn said. "What did that have to do with any of this? Besides making Amanda mad at me."

"That wasn't part of the plan."

"So, you have a plan," Finn said.

She grinned.

"Tell me," he said.

"It won't be easy," Storey said. "First, you're going to have to be honest. And that can be the hardest thing of all."

58

FINN ARRIVED AT the doors to Deck 4 a few minutes before eight. There was yellow tape blocking them. CLOSED FOR MAINTENANCE.

Several things struck him at once. If the walking track was closed, he and the dark fairy would need somewhere else to meet. If the sign was fake, then Maleficent had at least some of the crew working for her. She had closed off the deck to ensure no interference. He slipped through the doors, careful to keep the sign in place. He stepped outside.

The sea level had increased since dinner. He spread his legs to stabilize himself. Slapped in the face by a wet spray, he turned his back to the whitecaps. All alone on the deck, he looked both ways for any sign of Maleficent or his mom.

Maybe he'd walked into a trap. Maybe Luowski was about to beat up on Finn, steal the journal, and throw Finn overboard. It was either the high seas, the wind, or the shifting of the deck beneath his feet. But Finn was shaking.

She came out of the tunnel where the walking track

crossed the bow. Her black cape wrapped her like a cocoon. There was a small tear in it. He wanted to knock the horns off her green head. Her fingernails were white and as long as cat claws. Most of all, it was her smug look that frightened him. She had not a care in the world. She did not doubt her own success for a moment. She placed a hand onto her hip. Finn found the whole package intimidating.

"Glad you could make it," she said, still some distance from Finn.

"Where is she?" he called.

"I like that about you, Finnegan. Always so focused." She smiled, or tried to.

He held up the leather book he was carrying. "It goes over if I don't see her. If you try anything." He moved closer to the rail.

"Easy!" she called. Waving a hand, she sent a signal. Finn's mother came through a different set of doors closer to Maleficent.

"Mom!" Finn shouted.

"I wouldn't trust her!" Mrs. Whitman called out.

Maleficent twisted her wrist while pointing at Finn's mom. Mrs. Whitman bent and screamed with pain. The dark fairy released her, having made her point. "See?" she said loudly. "I can focus my energy as well." She found herself amusing.

"Change her back and send her toward me," Finn said.

"The record book first," Maleficent said.

"Not a chance." He swung the book over the railing, prepared to release it. Holding it there, he moved one stanchion closer to the dark fairy and his mother. He glanced quickly over the side. "Long way down," he said loudly. "Big waves tonight."

"Too bad your friends could not join you, Finnegan. Maybe you would have stood a chance. Then again, it is so hard when you have lied to them. Cheated them. I lie and cheat at will, you know? You ought to try it more often."

"She comes close enough that I can see her eyes change. If you've given her contacts to convince me, you might rethink that."

"Chicken and the egg," Maleficent said. "I only have the balcony reserved for a few minutes, Finnegan. You had better decide if you want this or not."

"Oh, I want this," Finn said. "But apparently, you don't." He let go of the journal. And it fell. Maleficent lurched, stumbled, and nearly tripped. Finn's mother ran toward him. The waves were too loud to hear it splash.

"You insolent, pathetic, malicious, spiteful little boy! What have you done?"

"Forced your green hand," Finn said.

"You have not a leg to stand on now. Think what you have just done!"

"You forgot brilliant and conniving," Finn said. He pulled his mother close and looked into her green eyes. *Come back!* he wanted to cry. He faced Maleficent. "The five pages are in my head. Memorized. Hurt me, kill me, and you've lost them for good."

She raised her hand malevolently. She intended to throw a spell.

"Think about that before you do something stupid!" He caught her, arm raised, neck strained, eyes bulging. "I know it word for word. Backward and forward. You kill me, it goes with me. You don't give me back my mother, it goes with me. With us." He pulled his reluctant mother to the railing with him. "Her eyes change now or forget our deal."

"I can get out of you anything that is in you," she said, a voice like sandpaper on stone.

"Free her."

"You will not jump," she said.

"You won't risk that." He backed up.

"Wait! Prove yourself." She flicked her wrist. A notebook hovered in the air before her, a pen upright on its page. "I shall take dictation. The first page, if you please."

228

"Free her," Finn repeated.

"I shall capitulate. The first paragraph, then." She rolled her neck on her shoulders. Finn heard pops and cracks over the sound of the waves. Tia Dalma strode out onto the deck. "Begin," Maleficent commanded.

Finn carefully recited the first paragraph from the journal's five well-worn pages. Tia Dalma listened intently.

Maleficent checked with the voodoo queen, who nodded. "Very good," Maleficent said, dripping in sarcasm.

"My mot—"

Maleficent interrupted. "First paragraph. Too easy. You must pass your A-Levels, you know? Page three, paragraph two."

Finn tried to picture the page, the paragraph. His nerves overcame him. He couldn't remember a thing.

Storey stepped onto the deck from the midships doors Finn had come through. She held up her hand toward the dark fairy.

"Who's this?" Maleficent questioned.

"If I may, your highness," Storey said.

Finn glared at Storey. *Your highness*. Storey was the double-cross. Not Maleficent. She moved toward Finn. He leaned back over the railing. Her eyes told him to trust her. His heart wouldn't allow it. She grabbed hold of Finn's hand. He tried to shake lose but she was abnormally strong.

Storey recited the passage from the journal.

Finn looked down at her holding his hand. Remembered her touching his face. "Psychometry," he said. "You can see through touch. You've stolen my thought."

Storey did not speak, did not defend herself. Finn could not trust her admonishing eyes. She was scolding him for what he'd said.

"Impressive," Maleficent said. "Both of you. Very impressive. So, he does have it memorized."

Storey nodded. "He does."

"Excellent."

"Release my mother now or I jump!"

"Such impatience!" Maleficent said. She waved a hand. The green in his mother's eyes dissolved.

"Finn!" Mrs. Whitman gasped. She looked around as if she had no idea where she was. "You," she said when she spotted Maleficent. "The beach. The woman selling hats."

"I do love a good role," Maleficent said. "And now, I'm sorry to say, I must take everything that's in your head." She raised both hands toward Finn.

Storey pushed Finn and Mrs. Whitman overboard.

She jumped to the railing and followed them over into the surging sea.

59

FINN HELD HIS mother's wrist tightly. The waves lifted and drove them both toward the hull of the ship. Just as they were to be smashed into the side, a strong current pushed off the hull. It drove them quickly toward the stern. Like the flume ride in Splash Mountain. They sank again. Finn kicked off his shoes and worked to tread water, refusing to let go of his struggling mother.

A hand caught hold of his belt. Storey's head bobbed in the waves. "Say it!" she cried out.

The next wave pushed them under again.

Finn released his breath in one massive exhale. "Starfish wise, starfish cries."

60

MAYBECK WIPED THE journal with an embroidered towel. A large fishnet lay on his bed. "That was an awesome catch, Charlie."

"Thanks." Charlene and Willa cuddled in an overstuffed chair from the suite's living room area. The chair faced Maybeck's bed, where he continued to dry the book. "He dropped it right where he said. Stanchion across from the doors. All I had to do was put the net in the right place."

"Even so, I would never have caught it. I'd have whiffed." The girls nodded. So did Philby at the computer.

"Did you see those porpoises?" Willa said. "It actually looked like they were smiling."

"They always look like that," Maybeck said.

"Do not," Willa said.

"That must have been some ride," Philby said from the computer. "Mrs. Whitman looked out of her mind with how much fun it was."

"Riding a porpoise? Who wouldn't like that? But pitch-dark, in waves like that? No thanks," said Charlene.

"Besides, Finn had no idea if the code would work. It was all on faith."

"He'd done it before," Maybeck said. He set down the journal. "All better," he said.

"You won't give him any credit, will you?" Charlene sounded incensed. "Everything he does, and still, you've got nothing good to say."

"At least I'm consistent," Maybeck snapped.

Charlene released an audible sigh. Maybeck broke into a smile. Everyone laughed.

61

FINN AND HIS MOTHER wore dry Cast Member clothing that had been delivered to them. They were in the Executive Officers' quarters, a small bedroom next to the captain's in a forward area of the ship where Finn had never been. The decision had been made to hide them until the ship made port the following morning.

"I think it's a mistake," his mom said. The decision had been made to fly home the parents of the Keepers. Having used Mrs. Whitman as leverage against Finn, the Overtakers threatened all the adults.

"Storey is eighteen. She will look after us. They'll move us to the crew quarters. We'll be safer there."

"I understand all that," his mother quipped. "You heard me. I agreed to the arrangements. Doesn't mean I like them."

"Show must go on," he said.

"I said I understand," she said. Her face softened. Her voice, too. "I also understand what you did for me, Finn. The risk you took. The risk you all took." He nodded. "You could have lost the journal. Lost everything."

"Storey claims that once she reads a person like that, she remembers what she sees."

"I know I'm supposed to believe she has that ability, but you'll excuse me if it's a little difficult for me."

"I didn't get it when she touched my face the other day. But she used it to learn that I'd given the journal to Philby. She then read Philby without him knowing about her ability. She saw where he'd hidden it."

"I still have to believe it's possible to do that."

"Yeah, I get it. The first time I crossed over I thought I was dreaming. When I saw Amanda use her *push* the first time, it was the same thing. Now not so much. I guess I don't really doubt that stuff. I kind of think anything is possible."

Her eyes crinkled. It meant she was happy. "That's a good way to be," she said. Her voice came out so softly Finn had to lean toward her. "Thank you for saving me." Tears formed. "That's hard for me to say. I'm your mother. *I'm* supposed to protect *you*."

"This time it was my turn," he whispered back. "We need each other, right?"

His mom squeezed his hand. She cried some more before wiping her eyes and blowing her nose. She smiled.

"You'll stay holograms now, whenever possible. What the captain recommended."

"It was Wayne's idea," Finn said. "He told the captain. But yes, that's the plan. And our programmed holograms will be giving tours and entertaining the passengers. Sticking to the schedule. So, there's that. The OTs won't know which one of us to attack. Diversion. Confuse your enemy. It's a good strategy."

"Listen to you." She cried some more. She must have been tired. "You're growing up too fast."

"I'm not sure that's possible. But I get it."

She laughed. That stopped the tears for good. "What am I going to do with you?"

He knew better than to answer that. She said it all the time.

That night they rode out the waves together. Neither slept well. Finn fell asleep around sunrise when the boat stopped rocking. A yellow glow kissed the horizon.

Later, he slipped out the door. Walked down the passageway to a set of stairs, at the bottom of which was a door, unmarked on the public side.

Amanda was sitting, her back to the wall of the corridor. A slight flicker told him it was her DHI, though he knew that was the only way she could be on the ship.

"Hey," Finn said. "You should have returned. It's way too late."

Her eyes were red. She stood. "If a hologram could hug a person, I would hug you."

"Okay," he said, not understanding.

"Charlie told me about you and Storey and I kind of flipped out. I should have been there to help you last night. I could have helped you."

"I get it," he said. "No big deal."

"You could have drowned."

"Other than that," he said. He won a smile from her.

"Friends?" she said.

"And then some," he said. It was the first time he'd said something like that to her. To any girl. He felt terrified. Foolish.

But then she nodded. "I'm glad."

When the ship was sailing, it emitted a deep hum from its belly. Finn felt it up his legs. Heard it in his bones. He liked cruising. He could get used to the lifestyle.

"Chernabog?" she asked.

"We told the captain. About Tia Dalma, too. They've searched the ship twice. Nothing."

"How's that possible?"

"How is any of this possible?"

"Magic." She nodded. "Yeah," she said. "She'll come after the journal again."

"Probably," Finn said. "Who knows? Maybe Chernabog flew off in the night. Maybe it's over. It doesn't matter. We kept the journal. My mom's okay."

"They'll be back," she said. "They always come back."

"Yeah," Finn said. A part of him felt so tired. Another part, excited. "We go through the canal. Belize. Mexico. It's going to be fun. You and Jess need to cross over earlier in the day. Join us for some of it."

Amanda nodded. "I'd like that."

"Or get Wayne to let you join the ship at the canal." He heard the excitement in his own voice. "I mean, if you and Jess would want to."

"I want to," she said. He wasn't sure that holograms could blush, but it looked like it. "They all came through for you."

"Yeah," he said.

"Because you told them the truth," she said. "That's a good thing."

"I was terrified," he said, admitting it. "That I'd been planning to betray them. That I'd kept secrets from them. It was awful."

"Not so bad," she said.

"I thought they would hate me. I thought you hated me."

Her eyes quieted. "As if that's ever going to happen."

They walked out to the deck and watched the sun clip the horizon. The seas had calmed. Land was in sight for the first time in days.

"I need to return me and Jess," Amanda said. "Mrs. Nash will be waking us up soon."

Finn waved his hand through her hologram. He laughed.

"What?" she asked.

"I've put my own hologram through things. But that's the first time I've done that. You know, being on the other side and all."

"Weird, right?" she said.

Finn nodded. "Definitely."

"Not as weird as this," she said. She pulled the Return out of her pocket.

She pushed the button.

ACKNOWLEDGMENTS (FIRST EDITION)

Special thanks to Chris Ostrander and Laura Simpson of Disney Synergy for connecting me with the wonderful people of the Disney Cruise Line including, in no special order, Karl Holz, Christian, Akim, Kevin, Angeline, Ray, James, Justine, Lisa, Michel, David, Mark, Aki, Sal, Tisa, Sarah (on Castaway Cay), Wilson, Zachary Alexander Wilson, "Uncle Bob," and Mark.

Thanks also to everyone at Disney Books, including Wendy Lefkon, Jessica Ward, Jeanne Mosure, Deborah Bass, and Jennifer Levine. And to John Horton at Disney's Youth Education Services for helping me create the Kingdom Keepers Quest in the Magic Kingdom.

I'm indebted to my office staff: Nancy Zastrow, Jenn Wood, and, for their copyediting skills, David and Laurel Walters and Judi Smith. My secret weapon is continuity reader Brooke Muschott, a walking, breathing Kingdom Keepers encyclopedia.

But in the end, the real acknowledgment must be to you, the Kingdom Keepers readers, who keep this series alive and make it so much fun to write. Thank you all.

GET A SNEAK PEEK OF
RIDLEY PEARSON'S NEW
KINGDOM KEEPERS BOOK

INHERITANCE

Coming in March 2022

1

ELI WHITMAN LIFTED HIS HANDS and screamed. He was sitting in the front row of Animal Kingdom's roller coaster, Expedition Everest. The thing was older than his parents! He could imagine the views from outside. Giraffes and hippos in the Kilimanjaro Safari. White seagulls perched atop the Tree of Life.

His friends cried out as the roller coaster dove. Parents weren't on the ride. Fine with him. At twelve and thirteen, he and his friends didn't need hand-holding.

As the roller coaster stopped, Eli had a brief view of Pandora, an attraction more than twenty years old. The Siberian Forest Climb and the Great Barrier Reach had opened two years earlier. That had been Animal Kingdom's fortieth birthday. Other kids might have gone there for a birthday party. Not Eli. Expedition Everest was his favorite. And this was, after all, his birthday party.

Animal Kingdom was super crowded. Tomorrow there would be a total solar eclipse. The Disney parks had special shows planned, including a Star Wars Sky Search.

When the roller coaster entered the double loop, Marie-Claire grabbed Eli's hand. She squeezed and held on tight. That made it the best day-before-his-birthday ever.

When he got off the ride, he stopped at the show wall to see a video of himself on the ride. The other kids looked strong or pretty. He saw himself as boring-looking. Freckles. Brown hair. Darkish skin. (His mother was part Asian; his father Caucasian.) In the video, the wind pushed back his hair. It gave away a secret: He kept his hair long to hide his gigantic ears.

The July air felt hot and damp. He was sweaty. Jungle trees and vines lined the path back toward the Monkey Temple. It was a place Eli liked to stop and watch for a while. He and Marie-Claire and a few other friends did just that. The sound of laughter filled the air. Happy birthday, he thought.

The group explored the rock canyons leading to Harambe. His parents had once tried to explain what the park had looked like back in 2020. But it was impossible for Eli not to see the solar holograms of the Disney Cast Members—Solograms—moving around throughout the park. He knew the hover carts were new. And so were attractions like Loch Ness Nessie, that he counted as favorites.

He knew he was lucky. Not everyone got to live in a

place like Epcot's CommuniTree. He had things others didn't. But he also wanted to travel more, like his parents did. They were currently riding the Hyperloop from Atlanta to Los Angeles. Instead of being with them, he was in the park. He had asked them if he could come along. His parents listened; they just didn't seem to ever hear him.

Maybe things would change tomorrow. Thirteen had to be better than twelve.

"Did you know that people in India don't eat during a solar eclipse because they think any food would be poisoned?" At ten, Lily Perkins was too young to hang out with sixth- and seventh-graders. There were unwritten rules about such things. But she was funny and smart, and she always made him feel better. To Eli, that was the definition of a good friend, and so he'd invited her.

"I did not," he admitted.

"In some cultures, pregnant women stay indoors during an eclipse." Her eye color matched her straight hair perfectly—brown with flecks of highlights in both. Her hair was very fine, and hung past her shoulders. She smiled for Eli and giggled, sounding like a complaining squirrel.

"Because?" he asked.

"Superstition." Lily wore a light blue V-neck pullover,

dandelion-yellow baggy cropped pants, and aquamarine retro-Moana flip-flops.

Eli's parents listened to extremely old music, including a singer named Stevie Wonder who'd written a pretty good song, "Superstition." The music started swirling in Eli's head and he felt his foot tapping. *Ver-y super-sti-tious.* He loved music. Any kind. But he didn't tell his friends that. So-called friends judged you on all kinds of stuff that shouldn't matter. He'd learned that the hard way.

"It's not all scary," Lily said. Thing about Lily: If you let her get going, it was hard to stop her.

"Is that so?" An only child, Eli was really nice to other kids, especially younger girls, whom he saw as little sisters. Like little Lily. Lily was the best, funniest, most unexpected creature on the planet.

"In Italy, some people think that flowers planted during a solar eclipse turn out more colorful than others. So, what do you think it means when a boy's thirteenth birthday is on the day of the solar eclipse?"

"I dunno," Eli said nervously.

"Maybe you'll grow a beard or something."

"Doubtful." Eli longed for the day he would start shaving.

"Maybe you'll start to age faster than everyone else your age."

"Now you're just being creepy," Eli said.

"Or find a princess." She giggled. "Other than Marie-Claire."

Eli swung to hit her playfully, but Lily saw and dodged the hit. Marie-Claire, who was French like her single mom, had transitioned from being Eli's science-class lab partner, to friend, to someone he now regularly texted with. The more they texted, the more Eli had trouble not texting her back. It was becoming a habit. If someone like little Lily had noticed, he had big problems.

"You know what I think?" Lily said.

"I'm not sure I want to." Eli hoped she would stop.

"I think you only wanted to ride Expedition Everest so Marie-Claire would freak out and hold your hand in the dark."

"Are you a mind reader?"

"Not exactly," Lily said sheepishly. "Kinda close, though." She giggled nervously.

Something about the way she said that interested Eli. He made a mental note to ask her more later.

"Keep that to yourself, will you, Lily?"

She ran off, skipping like a six-year-old. Eli smiled.